SCOUT
and the
RESCUE DOGS

SCOUT
and the
RESCUE DOGS

DIANNE WOLFER

Illustrated by
TONY FLOWERS

WALKER BOOKS
AND SUBSIDIARIES
LONDON • BOSTON • SYDNEY • AUCKLAND

Dianne is an active member of the Australian writing community. She supports local chapters of the Society of Children's Books, Writers and Illustrators, Story Dogs, and is a Room to Read Ambassador. Dianne is deeply grateful for support from the Western Australian Department of Local Government, Sport and Cultural Industries which allowed her valued research and writing time to complete an early draft of this story.

Scout and the Rescue Dogs
Walker Books Australia Pty Ltd
Locked Bag 22,
Newtown NSW 2042 Australia
www.walkerbooks.com.au

The moral rights of the author and illustrator have been asserted.

Text © 2025 Dianne Wolfer
Illustrations © 2025 Tony Flowers

All rights reserved. No part of this publication may be reproduced, stored in a retrieval system, or transmitted in any form or by any means – electronic, mechanical, photocopying, recording or otherwise – without the prior written permission of the publisher.

ISBN: 978 1 7616 0049 4

 A catalogue record for this book is available from the National Library of Australia

Typeset in 11 pt Stempel Garamond
Printed and bound in China

10 9 8 7 6 5 4 3 2 1

For Sophie, whose loss inspired the
Christmas letter, with truckloads of love.
And for Pete, the biggest spoiler of
our rescue dog, Harry.

– DW

CHAPTER 1 ESCAPING BOARDING SCHOOL 1

CHAPTER 2 LOST DOGS ONLINE 12

CHAPTER 3 FRIENDSHIP MESSAGES 21

CHAPTER 4 TUI AND TALISMANS 30

CHAPTER 5 TRAVELING ON 38

CHAPTER 6 SMOOTHING ROUGH EDGES 48

CHAPTER 7 TROUBLE IN EDEN 58

CHAPTER 8 MORE HOMES NEEDED 67

CHAPTER 9 STAR PRINCESS 77

CHAPTER 10 HIGH COUNTRY 86

CHAPTER 11 JAI AND THE PUGGLE 94

CHAPTER 12 WEBSITE PLANNING 105

CHAPTER 13 MEETING MOLLY 114

CHAPTER 14 TRUCKER BBQ 123

CHAPTER 15 CHRISTMAS 133

CHAPTER 16 NEW FRIENDS AND OLD FRIENDS 145

CHAPTER 17 TRUCKER AND DOG MATCHMAKING 154

CHAPTER 18 NEW YEAR FIRESTORM 166

CHAPTER 19 BURRUMBUTTOCK 174

CHAPTER 20 CORRYONG HAY RUN 183

CHAPTER 21 EMBER ATTACK 192

CHAPTER 22 A NEW START 204

PLACES SCOUT VISITS AND HEARS ABOUT......................... 210

CHAPTER 1
ESCAPING BOARDING SCHOOL

19 DECEMBER

Tick, tock, tick.

Scout stared at the classroom clock.

Ten to three.

Tick, tock, tick.

Five to three.

Tick, tock. *Briiing—*

She pushed her pencils and books into her bag.

"See you all next year." Ms Lawson opened the door. "Enjoy your holidays!"

Kids rushed out.

Scout grabbed her case from beside the locker. She clunked it down the stairs then steered its wobbly wheels across the yard of Arcadia Boarding School for Young Ladies. Outside the school gate, in the leafy upmarket street, parents were waiting by fancy cars. She pushed past them. Double-parked, at the end of the street, she could see a dusty green Kenworth truck. She quickened her pace, heading straight for the tall man standing beside it. He was scanning the crowd.

"Dad!" She let her case fall to the ground as she leaped into his arms. "I've been counting down all day."

"Me too." Dad hugged her tight. He tossed her case into the cabin as she climbed into Big Rig's passenger seat.

"Buckle up," he said. "We'll need to get moving if we're going to eat fish and chips on the beach at sunset."

"Yum." She clipped her seat-belt and kicked off her shoes. "It's so hot!" She wiggled her toes. "What are we hauling?"

"Fifty pallets of dog tucker."

"Whoa, that's a lot of dog food! And where are we heading?"

"South toward Melbourne then through the city to Frankston. There's a fish and chips van beside a truck-sized carpark near the pier. Hopefully it'll be cooler by the bay."

As he gunned the engine people turned to stare. Scout grinned. She loved the sound of Big Rig's motor. The steady boom was her earliest memory.

Dad tapped the steering wheel as they edged through the after-school traffic. Scout couldn't wait to get away. She'd had a terrible five months at her new school, and now to top it off, Ms Lawson wanted them to do an online friendship assignment over the summer break.

Her teacher had beamed as she said, "You might all find yourselves starting Year 7 with a new friend."

Scout didn't think so.

"We'll drop a pallet of food at Frankston Animal Shelter," Dad continued, "then have dinner by the pier. After that we'll stop overnight in a wayside on the way to Sale."

"Have I been to Sale?"

"We spent a weekend there, the summer before your mom was diagnozed."

"Oh." She gazed at the photograph of her mother glued onto the dashboard. It was surrounded by love hearts.

"Remember that video of you and Mom making a sandcastle?"

She nodded.

"That was taken at Ninety Mile Beach—it's near Sale."

"So can we go there first?"

"We can make a detour if you want to."

"And build another sandcastle?"

"You betcha!" Dad shifted the gearstick as Big Rig left the stop-start traffic and eased onto a feeder road.

As they merged into the slow lane on the Hume Highway, Scout cranked up the air-conditioner. "Why have we got so much dog food on board?"

"A philanthropist has donated it to animal shelters for Christmas."

"What's a philanthro . . ."

"Philanthropist. It's someone who does kind things with their money."

"That sounds fun. How do you get to be one?"

"Well, first you need to finish school and get a job to earn money to give away." Dad laughed. "And in the meantime, our 'kind thing' is spending the next five days delivering all this dog chow."

"Can I play with the rescue dogs?"

"That's the reason I volunteered for this job. When Mom promised you a pet for your birthday, we didn't think her cancer would return." He glanced at the photo on the dashboard. "If you can't have a dog of your own, I reckon the next best thing is visiting them. Your mom would've liked that."

Scout stared out the window. Before her eleventh birthday, she'd spent hours scanning dog rescue sites with Mom. They'd researched breeds and made a checklist of the best dog for them.

"A pet is for life," Mom used to say. "You can't rush into it."

The checklist was under Scout's pillow at home. Every day at boarding school she'd remembered that list, wishing she could turn back time, adopt an animal, and take it home. Finding the right dog might make up for not having the right human friend.

"You okay?" Dad checked the side mirror as another truck began overtaking.

"Yep." Now wasn't the right time to begin her Holiday Plan of convincing him not to send her back to Arcadia.

"Are *you* okay?" She glanced sideways.

"I'm all right. Just taking one day at a time."

Scout leaned forward to look at Dad's GPS. "Can I double-check the traffic on my phone map?"

"Just the traffic!"

Getting a phone before going to Arcadia was the only good thing about boarding school. Dad had written a list of rules about using it, including times she could text and only contacts he knew—

"All clear until the outskirts of Melbourne," she announced, "but I'll keep you updated." She reached under the seat for her favorite driving cap. Its possum eyes twinkled above the visor and small ears stretched as she pulled it onto her head.

"Beauty," Dad said. "I love having my favorite possum ride shotgun. Did you hear any good jokes this term?"

Scout shook her head. He was the king of corny jokes. "I don't want to encourage you."

"Hey, dad jokes are no laughing matter!" He beamed. "Get it?"

Scout groaned.

The CB radio crackled and she reached for the handset.

"Big Rig, over," she said.

"G'day, Big Rig. It's Sal here in Firebird. Hey, Bill, have you collected that precious cargo? Over."

"Hello, Aunty Sal, it's me, Scout, and yes, Dad's picked me up. Now we're heading south, not far from Seymour. Where are you?"

"On your tail, buddy. I've just left Benalla."

"Where are you heading?"

"Bendigo—how about you?"

"Dad's taking me for fish and chips at the Frankston Pier, then we're driving east to deliver dog food to animal shelters."

"Sounds like fun. Have a potato cake for me and I'll see you next week at the Christmas barbecue in Barnawatha."

"Okay. And, Aunty Sal, guess what? Over."

"What?"

"I've grown an inch since last holiday, so I reckon I might be taller than you now."

"We'll see about that. Hugs for now. Over."

Scout replaced the handset and turned up the radio. A reggae version of "The Little Drummer Boy" was playing. She tapped the beat then joined Dad to chant the chorus.

"Pa rum pum pum pum, Rum pum pum pum, Rum pum pum pum . . ."

For six wonderful weeks she was free. Well, after she completed Ms Lawson's friendship assignment, she would be. She took a notebook out of her bag. Might as well get started.

"What are you doing?"

"Ms Lawson's worried about class bullying, so she's given us a Christmas project."

"Are you being bullied?"

Scout hesitated. Did having no friends at school and being ignored count as bullying?

"No." She kept her eyes on the road.

"Good. So what's the project?"

"It's a bit like an online Secret Santa. Tomorrow we'll get an email from Ms Lawson on the School-to-Family Intranet. There'll be three names in the email. We're meant to send each person a message saying something positive."

"That sounds fun."

"Hmm, it depends which names she sends, and whether anyone gets back to me. Ms Lawson says it's not 'compulsory' but that she'll be 'delighted' if we all take part."

Dad chuckled. "She's a cracker, that Ms Lawson."

"What does that mean?"

"That she's smart."

Scout grabbed a pen from the door pocket. Between road bumps she tried to list nice things about her classmates. For some it was challenging.

She wrote positive words like "creative," "logical," "friendly," and "generous." Then she hesitated. What words did other girls her age want to be? "Popular", "pretty," "pouty?" She wasn't sure. Dad often told her she was kind, and Mom used to say she was great at finding patterns. They'd loved collecting rocks and insects together. Scout chewed the end of her pencil. What words described that: "observant," "curious?" Those were positive things for her family and kids at her old bush school, but at Arcadia, pretending to be well-off or grown-up seemed more important. She'd found that the only way to make friends was by trying to be like the popular girls. That was too high a price for her.

As Big Rig rumbled down the highway, she checked Dad's phone. Making a playlist was way more fun than worrying about her stuck-up classmates.

Dad used the CB radio to check traffic updates with other truck drivers.

"End of term, mate, all roads are busy—"

"It's crowded today."

At Craigieburn they turned onto the M2 and drove through Melbourne's peak-hour traffic. Big Rig's air brakes hissed and squeaked as commuters ducked in front of them like bumper cars.

"What time does the first animal shelter close?" Scout re-checked the route on her phone. "We might not make it."

"Let's give it our best shot. If we can do one drop-off today, that'll give us more time to get to the next shelter at Sale tomorrow."

The M2 became the M1. Traffic crawled. Dad's fingers drummed the steering wheel. After passing a big shopping center they turned onto the M3 and he moved up a few gears.

Scout rang the shelter to let them know they were on their way. Voicemail answered.

"You have called outside office hours. Please contact us again between eight am and five pm. If your matter is urgent you can call the council ranger."

"They're closed."

"Never mind, Possum," Dad said. "There's a truckers' rest area behind a station near the animal shelter. Not my favorite place to overnight, but it'll do. Then we can be at the shelter bright-eyed and bushy-tailed when they open at eight."

"Okay." She pressed "end route" on Dad's GPS. "Where to now – fish and chips at Frankston Pier?"

"Yep." His belly grumbled. "Don't know about you, but I'm ready for a feed."

After a few more traffic lights, he pointed ahead. "Almost there. That parking area has boat trailer bays. It's not far from the pier."

"And I can see a fish and chip van."

Dad maneuvered the rig into a long trailer bay. While he made sure their load hadn't shifted, Scout searched for interesting rocks. She picked up a few stones with promising patterns and speckles. They'd need to be polished in her tumbler before she knew what they were like inside, but surprise discoveries were the best part of being a rock hound.

"All secure."

She put her stones inside the truck cabin, then they went to order.

"There's a twenty-minute wait."

"No worries." Dad tapped his card. "We'll stretch our legs."

They wandered over to a giant crab sculpture and Scout did handstands on the grass around it. "Look how much my cartwheels have improved!"

"Dead set legend." He grinned as her cap went flying.

They ate on the beach surrounded by squawking gulls. Dinner was perfect. Hot, salty, and not too greasy. Scout adjusted her cap and took a potato cake selfie for Aunty Sal, then they strolled along the pier. She skipped ahead to watch an old man reel in a fish. She sighed. Boarding school was over sixty miles away and if she didn't count missing Mom and wishing for a best friend to share adventures with, then things were okay.

Dad caught up with her and they linked arms.

"I did hear one funny joke," she said, "and it's even about dogs."

"I'm listening."

"The police say that someone's been stealing their sniffer dogs, but it's all right—" She paused. "They have several leads."

"Oh no." He laughed. "That's too corny—even for me!"

CHAPTER 2
LOST DOGS ONLINE

Scout scrambled into the passenger seat with a full tummy. They drove for twenty minutes then Dad pulled up beside another truck at the back of a twenty-four hour roadhouse. As he checked Big Rig's tyre pressure she climbed into the space behind the front seats. She pulled down the window blinds to block the flashing Christmas lights and noticed something on her bunk.

"You packed my tumbler," she cried.

"I knew my little geologist would be searching for treasures along the way."

"Thanks, Dad."

She changed into pajamas, brushed her teeth then snuggled under a sheet on the top bunk. Big Rig's cabin was like a safe cocoon. She wondered if caterpillars felt this cosy before they became butterflies.

"How far is it to the shelter we're visiting in the morning?"

"Just a few miles down the road."

"Can I look for it on my phone?"

"Just maps!"

Searching for the shelter was easy. She showed Dad the website and they clicked on the link. Dozens of dog photos popped up. She scrolled through, putting love hearts beside her favorites. Poppy the black labradoodle was the cutest.

"I can't wait to meet you tomorrow," Scout whispered. She blew Poppy a kiss, turned off the phone and then read for a while.

"Lights out," Dad said.

She closed her eyes. Falling asleep to the hum of traffic and his snores felt like being wrapped in a favorite blanket. Scout curled up and drifted away.

She woke to sunshine streaming through the windscreen and the sound of magpies warbling. She counted caroling patterns between warbles, then watched a bird pecking Big Rig's side mirror. It thought its reflection was another bird.

Dad walked across the carpark, balancing coffee and hot chocolate. She opened the truck door and he handed up her keep-cup. "What would you like for breakfast, Possum?"

"Can you do golden syrup and banana porridge?"

"Sure can."

The cabin had a tiny fridge, microwave and sink. He measured out oats and water into bowls, then put them in the microwave while Scout arranged camping chairs next to Big Rig's front wheels. This was a perfect time to start her Holiday Plan. Step One: make Dad understand how unfriendly Arcadia was.

"This is so yummy," she mombled between mouthfuls. "The porridge at boarding school tastes like Play-Doh."

"That good, hey." Dad sipped his coffee. "Do you know how Reese eats her porridge?"

Scout thought for a moment. "Witherspoon?"

"You're a chip off the old block." He winked.

Dad seemed to have missed the point. She frowned, climbed back into the cabin and flicked on the radio while she washed their dishes.

"Now here's a fun Christmas carol for you to sing along to," the announcer said.

"Feliz Navidad, Feliz Navidad—"

Scout dropped the spoon she was drying. "Feliz Navidad" was her mom's favorite carol. Every December she'd played it while they decorated their Christmas tree. Scout even knew the words in Spanish so she could Skype-sing with her grandmother.

Dad climbed up the steps. "You okay?" he asked softly.

She nodded and brushed away her tears.

They tidied the bunks, then drove to the dog shelter. A chubby fellow in a black and white footy vest was opening the gates as they pulled up. Despite the heat he wore a beanie in matching Collingwood club colors.

"G'day." He shook Dad's hand. "I'm Tony. Thanks for bringing all this food."

"No worries, Tony. Where do you want me to stack it?"

"By the office door would be good."

Dad set up his ramps, unhooked Big Rig's forklift and shifted two pallets to the entry.

There were four boxes on each pallet and each box held six bags. Scout did a quick calculation: eight boxes times six made forty-eight bags, each holding thirty-three pounds.

"Fifteen hundred and eighty-four pounds of dog food," she announced as the men stacked the boxes.

"Is that so?"

"She's a whiz at maths." Dad grinned.

Tony laughed. "Want to meet some of the dogs?"

"Is Poppy here?" said Scout. "I saw her on your website."

"Oh—Poppy? That big sweetheart was adopted weeks ago. Sorry, love, we're way behind with updating our dog profiles. A volunteer comes in when she can to post the ones who've been adopted and to add new dogs to the website. Last time I tried to do it, I lost half the photos."

He opened the doors to the kennel and shouted, "G'day, everyone!" Dogs of all shapes and sizes woofed and scratched at their cages. "Behave yourselves." He put on a serious face. "We have visitors."

Scout went from cage to cage, greeting the dogs, holding her hand against the mesh for them to lick, and trying to pat them through the wire. There were nine, but she'd only seen two of them on the website.

Tony fed the dogs then let them run in the yard. As Scout played with two bouncy pups, she had an idea.

"Would you like me to update the photos?" She tickled one pup's tummy. "I know how to edit websites."

Tony leaned against his broom.

"That'd be beaut." He nodded. "If we get their details online, these doggies'll have a better chance of being adopted. Some might even find forever homes before Christmas."

"Do we have time, Dad?"

He checked his watch. "The shelter at Sale is two and a half hours away and they're not expecting us till early afternoon. Could you do it in forty minutes?"

"No problem."

"Alright, I'll help Tony clean the cages while you get cracking—"

Scout jumped up. "What's the log-in password?"

Tony rummaged in a drawer, then handed her a sheet of paper. "It's all on there," he said.

Scout went straight to work. She took photos of each dog, using treats to get cute expressions, then she logged onto the shelter's website. Removing dogs that had been adopted was easy, but adding new bios took longer.

"Can you tell me a few things about each dog?"

Tony took off his beanie and scratched his head. "Well, let's start with Alfred. He's a majestic boy and a bit of a joker. He doesn't like kids, probably got teased in the past. Then there's Billy. He's anxious, but he means well. Ginger loves everyone. She's good with kids and other dogs. Nellie's gentle. She'd do best with someone calm. Tiny and Puddles are best mates. They're always together so it'd be beaut if one family took them both. Freckles and Speckles are from the same litter. Their other sister was adopted yesterday and Dotty's their mom. Poor old girl. She's had way too many pups, by the look of her."

"Thanks, Tony."
Scout's fingers flew over the keyboard.

ALFRED:

Everyone at the shelter loves this majestic boy. Alfred is as clever as Einstein, but he's had a bad experience with children. This chap needs an adults-only home.

BILLY:

Billy is a nervous boy who's had a rough start in life. He hopes to find a special someone who will take him to puppy school and be patient with him.

GINGER:

Ginger is a stylish girl. She gets on well with children, other dogs, and even cats! Ginger loves cuddles. Could she be your new bestie?

"I'm nearly done!" Scout typed faster as Dad checked his watch.

NELLIE:

Nellie is sweet, and enormous! She loves having her ears stroked and is looking for a calm family where she can feel safe.

TINY AND PUDDLES:

Do you have a big yard? Tiny and Puddles love running and they give the best slobbery kisses. Can you give these boy buddies their forever home?

FRECKLES AND SPECKLES:

If you're ready for a high energy friend or double-trouble, come and meet this cuddly pair. Hurry, these bouncy pups won't be here for long. One male, one female.

DOTTY:

Dotty is a gentle girl who's had many pups and now needs quiet 'you-and-me-time'. Are you able to adopt her?

"Blimey," Tony muttered when she'd finished. "You're a right legend, girl."

Scout beamed. Now all the dogs had a better chance of finding forever families.

"We'd better get moving," Dad said. "It's almost ten o'clock."

After a final goodbye to the dogs, Scout climbed into the cabin.

"Cheers," Tony yelled over the rumble of Big Rig's engine. "Have a ripper Christmas!"

"You too!"

As Scout waved from the window her dad reached across to squeeze her hand.

"That was a kind thing to do," he said. "I'm proud of you."

CHAPTER 3
FRIENDSHIP MESSAGES

"Want one?" Dad offered Scout a mint as they turned onto the Princes Highway and headed east. "There's a nice station at Rosedale with plenty of parking space. How about we stop there for lunch?"

"Okay, then how long to the next animal shelter?'

"Only half an hour after Rosedale. If we arrive before one o'clock we'll have plenty of time to visit Ninety Mile Beach."

"Sounds good."

"Rightio. Now, if you want to borrow my noise-canceling headphones to listen to your music, then I'll listen to my whodunit audio book."

Scout opened her phone and chewed her mint as she scrolled through her Christmas playlist. As they drove east, she thought about Tony and the rescue dogs. If Dad let her have one, which would she choose?

The suburbs soon became paddocks. Then they passed a huge open-cut mine and power plants near Yallourn and Morwell.

"What do you call a power failure?" Dad said at the end of a chapter.

"Hmm, I don't know."

"A current event."

Scout thought for a few minutes. "What did the baby light bulb say to the mommy light bulb?"

"You are the light of my life?"

"Good try." Scout laughed. "But no."

"Okay, I give up."

"I love you watts and watts."

Dad gave a little toot of the air horn. "Excellent," he said. "I'll have to remember that one for Theo. He loves hearing new jokes."

"Can we turn up the air-conditioning? I'm boiling."

"Okay, Meaty Bites aren't heavy, so I reckon Big Rig can handle some air-con drag."

Scout tucked her ponytail under her cap and switched the dial to high, while Dad tuned the radio.

"As we go to news, the record-breaking heat wave continues across Australia. Catastrophic fire conditions are expected for Sydney and surrounding areas. A massive blaze is raging near the town of

Bargo. Fires are being driven by strong winds and several firefighters have been injured."

"Poor fellows," Dad muttered. "We're in for a horror bushfire season with everything so dry."

"Meanwhile, South Australia has reported a fifth fire emergency with two out-of-control blazes on Kangaroo Island. In Victoria, sweltering conditions continue across the state with a cool change possible later today."

"Let's flippin' hope so!"

"And in sport—" He turned up the volume. "The Hobart Hurricanes play the Sydney Sixers this afternoon. Then at 6.10, the Brisbane Heat play the Melbourne Stars at Metricon Stadium."

"Go, Stars!" he shouted.

Scout wasn't a cricket fan. She closed her eyes and thought about home. Only four more sleeps till they were back at their little farm near Beechworth. She imagined her room, the animal wall posters and her microscope bench. Then she wondered what was happening with the class friendship project.

"Can I use my phone to check for school emails, Dad?"

"Okay."

She typed in the family password and opened her inbox. There was an email from Ms Lawson. She clicked on the message and groaned. The first two names for the friendship assignment were Ava and Sienna, the most popular girls. Scout remembered her second day at boarding school, when they'd caught her sobbing in the bathroom. As she wiped away her tears, they'd raised their pretty eyebrows, whispered "cry-baby" and raced down the hallway.

As she went back to class, Scout heard them giggling. She blushed and one of the kinder girls said, "Are you okay?"

Scout couldn't answer. She missed home and her old friends. There were no words to explain the sadness and fear of a future without Mom.

Over the following week, she'd worked hard at being invisible. Soon most of the girls seemed to decide she was either weird or a loner. They left her alone. Only Sienna and Ava continued the sniping. They called her "cry-baby," and "ginger," then after her birthday they added "geek-freak" to their teasing.

That nickname had started when she tried just once to avoid being invisible. It was her birthday. She'd invited three girls to her room for a geode-smashing celebration. The girls were wary at first as they gathered around the rocks that Aunty Sal had sent.

"Far out!", they gasped as Scout used a small mallet to crack one open. She showed her classmates the crystal hidden inside. After smashing the first geode they couldn't wait to crack more. The geodes were mostly white quartz, but there were a few pinks as well. When the smashing was done, she shared some chocolates she'd been saving.

Later on, Sienna heard about the party she hadn't been invited to. She sneered at the girls who had been invited, tossed her hair and said, "Rocks are boring."

The other girls fidgeted, hesitated, then agreed. After that, Scout kept her science projects to herself.

She peered across at Dad. Step Two of her Holiday Plan was telling him that whenever she felt sad or lonely, she imagined she was at home in her old bedroom, surrounded by rocks, shells, special leaves, and family photos. She wanted to explain that when she closed her eyes, the bleak boarding school walls morphed into her leafy tree-house, and that Sam from next door was calling her to come and see a bird's nest—

"Idiot!" Dad growled as a car cut in front of them.

Hmm, perhaps this wasn't the right time for Step Two. Scout glanced back at the screen, read the names on her friendship list again, and wondered whether Ms Lawson knew what had been going on with Ava and Sienna. Why had she given her their names? They probably wouldn't bother sending her a message.

And if they did, would it be something mean?

She drafted a sarcastic message in her mind:

> Hi Ava,
> I like the way you are so kind to new girls—

She grinned. But this was meant to be a friendship assignment. Delete.

> Hi Ava,
> I like the way you braid your hair. It looks really nice.
> Best wishes,
> Scout

She pressed *Send* and stared at Sienna's name. Sienna was even more of a challenge. What nice thing could she say about someone who persuaded others to do mean things, then slunk into the shadows while her schemes were carried out?

> Hi Sienna,
> You have such a talent for teasing people and you are so skilful at being cruel. Thanks for making my time at Arcadia totally miserable.
> Geek-Freak-Ginger

Her finger hovered above the *Send* button, then she remembered Mom's words: sarcasm is the lowest form of wit. She took a deep breath and was about to delete her nasty words when Big Rig hit a pothole.

"Whoa, that was a big one!" Dad gripped the wheel, then turned his head. "Sorry, I couldn't avoid it."

Scout stared at the screen. The message had been sent. "Oh no."

"You okay?"

"Umm—yes."

She imagined Sienna reading the message. Despite the heat she broke into a cold sweat. She rummaged in her school bag for Ms Lawson's instructions. Oh no, it was worse. Ms Lawson was the moderator checking messages. She would be the one who read the mean words. Scout tried desperately to retrieve the email, but it was too late. Her cheeks felt hot and she quickly changed the message.

> Hi Sienna,
> I think you are really clever, way more than some people know.
> Have a happy Christmas,
> Scout

Was that positive enough? She chewed her lip and read the message again. For Sienna it was the best she could do.

She pressed *Enter*. Maybe Ms Lawson would read the latest message first and ignore the bad one. She crossed her fingers, feeling like the meanest girl on the planet.

The third name on her list was better. Anika was an enigma. She helped in the library and whenever she saw Scout, she smiled and said hi. Scout studied her list of positive things and typed out a longer message.

Hello Anika,
I don't know you well, but you seem thoughtful and I think we both love reading because I see you in the library. My positive project thing about you is that, even though I'm not great at sport, I really like it that you are.
At the moment I'm traveling with my dad. He's a truck driver and we're delivering food to animal shelters. It's fun.
I hope you're enjoying the holidays.
See you,
Scout

As the words whooshed from her outbox, she leaned back, surprised that writing the last message had sparked a small feeling of belonging, something she'd never felt before at Arcadia. She remembered all the times she'd hidden in the library at lunchtime. Maybe she could ignore Ava and Sienna and learn to be braver. That is, if she ever went back to Arcadia ...

"Are you okay?" Dad frowned.

"Yep," she said. "You're right: Ms Lawson is smart!"

He reached for his water bottle, looking puzzled as he turned off the highway into the Rosedale roadhouse.

While he ordered, Scout searched for rocks. An unusual one glinted at the edge of the carpark. She picked it up and whispered, "Thanks, Mom."

They sat on a bench under some trees. There was a smoky smell from small bushfires in the region. "Let's keep moving," Dad muttered. "It feels like the weather's turning. The sooner we get to Sale, the better."

CHAPTER 4
TUI AND TALISMANS

Big Rig's air brakes hissed and they shuddered to a stop outside the animal shelter. Scout opened her door and stepped into a blast of hot air. She wiped her forehead as a young woman in rainboots unlocked the door.

"Hi, I'm Tui. Are you the dog food people?"

"That's us. I'm Bill and this is my daughter, Scout."

"Thanks for coming." Tui gave them a double thumbs-up. "You guys are lifesavers. Our food stocks are really low and we had no idea how we'd get through Christmas. Then you emailed!"

"Well, let's get these boxes off the truck and into your cupboards," Dad suggested. "While I organize the forklift, perhaps Scout can help feed the animals or clean cages."

"That'd be great."

Scout followed her through the office, trying not to stare at the stingray tattoos covering her arms.

"It's a menagerie here," Tui warned. "Let's start with the dogs. Once they've eaten we can let them run in the yard."

There were six of them: three kelpie pups, a mastiff cross, a heeler, and an old spaniel named Archie. Scout loved them all.

They spooned food into six bowls and she put one inside each cage. Keeping the pups apart was tricky. Once the dogs were fed, she chopped carrots for some rabbits and fed kibble to a huge marmalade cat. Then she helped Tui hose out the dog pens, enjoying the occasional splash of cool water on her face. She worked quickly, hoping she'd have time to play with the puppies. Meanwhile Dad stacked the dog food.

"What about an iced tea before you go, Bill?"

"That's a beaut idea, thank you."

Tui and Dad talked about spot fires and changing winds, while Scout threw sticks for the heeler and cuddled the puppies. She held the tiniest pup close to her face. The squirmy bundle smelt like summer sunshine.

"I wish I could keep you," she said, but she knew that was impossible.

"The kelpies are from one of those puppy farms." Tui came over and sat beside her. "Poor little things. Before they arrived, their paws had never touched grass."

"Why?"

"Some breeders don't follow the rules. They keep mothers in cages, having litter after litter. Overbreeding is illegal, but it's hard to catch them. They sell the pups when they're very young."

Scout shuddered and held the pup closer.

"The shelters along the south coast have a network to report suspicious behavior, but the puppy farmers are sneaky." Tui handed Scout a card with her name and email on it. "If you see anything that concerns you on your travels, let me know and I'll tell the RSPCA. We need all the help we can get."

"Okay."

Dad checked the tyres while Scout took photos of the dogs. Maybe she could be an animal photographer when she left school, as well as a philanthropist. The pictures were cute. If anyone from school did write to her, at least she'd have something interesting to show them.

As Tui led the older dogs back to their cages, Scout stroked the tiny pup's ears. She closed her eyes, remembering the dog wish-list under her pillow at home.

"I know what it's like to live somewhere strange, too," she told the pup, "although at boarding school I don't sleep in a cage." The kelpie licked her hand as she described her farm bedroom. "There are posters on the walls, and under my pillow there's a best-dog-for-me checklist. Mom was allergic to fur, so no-shedder and low-shedder breeds were in the top spots on the list: poodle, schnauzer, bichon frise. We thought a kelpie might have too much energy, but you seem pretty calm."

Tui came back to collect the puppy. "He's sweet, isn't he? Would your dad let you take him?"

"I don't think so," Scout whispered. Tui was nice, but she didn't want to tell her about the list and how her mother had been helping her choose the right dog for their family.

"That's okay. He's not toilet trained. I guess that might be tricky in a truck cabin."

They laughed and Scout peeked at Tui's neck tattoo.

"It's a stingray," she said, lifting her hair. "See how it winds behind my ears."

"Did it hurt when you had it done?"

"Yeah, neck skin is sensitive, hey, but having it there reminds me to be brave."

"It's beautiful."

"Thanks."

"I need something to make me brave," Scout mombled, "but Dad would hit the roof if I got a tattoo!"

"You seem brave to me."

"I used to be. Now the girls at my boarding school call me 'geek' and 'cry-baby'." Tears welled up in her eyes as if to prove them right. She blinked them away.

"Geeks are awesome and being sad doesn't mean you're not brave." Tui held onto the pup as it wriggled in her lap. "Look." She showed Scout a greenstone necklace. "This is the bird that I'm named after, but sometimes the greenstone makes me sad because I miss my home in Rotorua."

"New Zealand?"

"That's right."

"I've never seen greenstone before." Scout reached out to touch the necklace. "I polish rocks. My tumbler's in the truck."

"Cool."

"And I'm named after a bird too," Scout whispered. "Well, sort of—my mom's favorite book was *To Kill a Mockingbird* and the girl in that is called Scout."

"Mockingbirds are clever. They mimic other birds. Where's your mom now?"

"She died last June."

"No wonder you're sad. Did the girls at school know?"

Scout shook her head.

"They might have been nicer if you'd told them."

"Having them gossip about Mom would have been worse."

Tui squeezed her hand. "There were girls like that at my school. Ignoring them worked best for me."

Scout blinked again.

"Does your dad know about the mean girls?"

"I don't want to worry him," Scout said. "He's sad too, but I'm trying to convince him not to send me back to boarding school."

"Good luck with that," Tui said, "and in the meantime, maybe you'll find a special stone to make into a mockingbird necklace."

"I don't think we have mockingbirds in Australia."

"Magpies and lyrebirds are good mimics. They're similar."

"I heard magpies this morning."

"There you go. And even if it isn't a bird, I have a feeling that soon you'll find a talisman of your own, one that reminds you how strong you are."

"What's a talisman?"

"Something that you treasure, like a lucky charm."

"Sometimes I find special leaves or stones," Scout hesitated, "and it kind of feels like Mom has helped me find them."

"Maybe she has."

The pup wriggled into her lap and chewed the top of Tui's gumboot.

"Do you have a favorite color?" Tui said. "Mine's green. It means balance."

"Because it's near the middle of the visible light spectrum."

"That's right." Tui was impressed. "And I guess being in the middle of the rainbow does work well for me. What's yours?"

Scout thought for a moment. "I used to like purple, but now my favorite is blue, next to you on the color band."

"Blue's about trust and speaking your truth."

Scout thought about that as Dad walked over to join them. He stopped at the heeler's cage.

"Poor fella. You should be out running in a paddock."

"This is Fly," Tui said. "His owner had an accident and can't look after him. He said leaving Fly was breaking his heart, but that he had no choice. I've been trying to find a special family who can adopt him, but no luck yet."

Dad reached through the bars to stroke the heeler's ears. "Sorry we can't take you, Fly, but good luck finding a kind home." Then he turned to Scout. "All ready to go?"

"Yep." She gave the kelpie pup one last hug, then waved to its brothers.

"It was nice to meet you," Tui said. "Thanks for your help and don't forget there are lots of ways to be brave."

Scout nodded and climbed into Big Rig.

As Dad steered out of the yard, Tui waved. She was tall and strong. Scout would never have guessed she needed a tattoo to remind her to be brave.

"You're quiet," Dad said. "A penny for your thoughts."

"Things are not always what they seem," she said, looking out the window.

He laughed as Big Rig rumbled out onto the Princes Highway. "I didn't expect that," he said as she opened her phone to check for messages.

She scrolled up and down. There were no friendship replies yet.

CHAPTER 5
TRAVELING ON

"How much further?"

"A while still."

The detour to Ninety Mile Beach was twenty-one miles each way. Dad listened to Big Bash cricket while Scout rested her head on the window. She tried to remember the time they'd been here as a family. A few images flashed in her mind, but she wondered whether they were real memories or memories from photographs.

Halfway to the beach they caught up to a trailer wobbling along at forty-five miles per hour. Scrawled across the back were the words, "Betty and Doug looping around Australia!"

"It's going to be a very slow loop." Dad shifted down through the gears.

Scout didn't mind going slower; she was watching pelicans soar in thermals. She rested her elbows on the window and saw a tiny bush school tucked back from the road. "Hey, that looks like my old school." She remembered her Holiday Plan and added, "Small schools are the best!"

Dad raised his eyebrows. "We're nearly there. Look out for somewhere to park."

"How about over on that reserve?"

"Beauty."

They changed into swimsuits, sun-blocked, and locked up Big Rig. Dad pointed to a sandy track at the end of the street. They followed it to a beautiful wide beach.

"It hasn't changed." He looked happy *and* sad.

Scout hugged him and dumped her towel. "Race you in."

They ran across blistering sand and splashed into the sea. After catching a few waves together, Scout floated on her back, looking up at the clouds, wondering about Mom. After the funeral Dad had said, "She'll always be with us in spirit." Was she here now?

Scout closed her eyes and felt the ocean rock her gently.

"All okay out there?" Dad called from the beach, where he was spreading out their towels. She waved and swam to shore, then they lay back, listening to waves shush across the sand.

"I miss Mom."

"Me too, Possum." Dad put his arm round her. "I think about Molly every day." He squeezed Scout's hand. "And then I bless my stars that I have you."

Pelicans soared above them as they spoke about the time before. Scout leaned against Dad. Talking about Mom was sad, but it was better than not talking about her at all.

"I hate being at boarding school," she whispered, "away from home and family memories."

"I know. You've been a trooper."

"I wish things could be the way they were."

"Me too, little Scout, but they can't be." He reached out a hand. "Come on, Trooper, we'd better get cracking if we're going to build this monster sandcastle."

"Okay."

Scout sighed. Telling Dad she didn't want to be at Arcadia wasn't working very well so far.

Dad pushed sand into a pyramid shape while she scooped up sloppier sand from the sea. She drizzled it over the pyramid and as the castle grew, they added turrets and a moat. She dredged a channel to the water so the moat could fill.

When the sandcastle was finished, Dad drew love hearts in the sand and Scout used a stick to write,

"I miss you, Mom." Then they posed for selfies in front of their masterpiece. Scout kept the best one as a screensaver.

Before leaving, they walked along the wide beach, looking for shells. Scout scuffed through the sand and her big toe bumped what looked like a scallop. She washed off the grit. The ridges of the crimson shell reminded her of Mom's hand before she'd died. It was so thin that each metacarpal bone stood out. She stroked the shell. There were no chips. It was perfect.

"A talisman," she murmured. Maybe Mom had wanted her to find it.

She showed Dad.

"That's a beauty." He found a shell of his own and when they got back to Big Rig he put it on the dashboard near Mom's photo. Scout kept her scallop shell tucked away in her pocket.

Bairnsdale Animal Shelter was the next stop. It was less than an hour's drive. The dogs there had found homes, but the volunteers were glad to receive food ahead of the after-Christmas rush.

"Why is there a rush after Christmas?" Scout said to the manager.

"Some people buy puppies as presents." He shook his head. "Then a few weeks after Christmas, when they realize how much time it takes to look after a dog, they dump them. Other people don't want to pay boarding fees, so they bring their animals here before going on holidays."

"That's terrible."

"It is, isn't it?"

"Do you have any dogs from puppy farms?"

"Not at the moment. Why?"

"There were rescue kelpies at the animal shelter in Sale. They came from a puppy farm and the girl there asked me to keep a lookout for others."

"Was that Tui? We worked with her on an RSPCA raid last year. We saved fifteen dogs. They were training the bigger pups for dog fights."

How could some humans be so cruel?

Dad checked his watch. "Time to go."

"Where to next?"

"Eden. It'll take about four hours. First thing tomorrow we can drop food at the shelter there. After that we'll have a rest day."

They waved goodbye to the Bairnsdale volunteers and Scout checked the map as he accelerated and worked up through the gears.

The Princes Highway snaked through thick

conservation forest. She opened the window as Big Rig passed creeks named after wombats and bellbirds, but the air was too smoky to enjoy. She watched trees whizz past instead, and tried to calculate the average number of leaves on each branch. She remembered reading that gum leaves grow in pairs on opposite sides of a stem, and that neighboring leaf pairs are at right angles, but that didn't help her guess the number of leaves. There could be thousands. Perhaps if she worked out how many were on each twig she could do it.

Dad pulled off the road at Cann River. "This place has good coffee," he said. "Let's stop and stretch our *pegs*."

Scout set aside her leaf guessing, jumped out, and searched the carpark for rocks. There weren't many, but she popped a few into her pockets. Sometimes the ugliest ones turned out to be the best.

Dad ordered coffee for himself and a milkshake for her. It was spearmint, her favorite flavor. She took a huge sip and the icy milk gave her a brain freeze.

The air was hazy so they didn't stay long.

"Why did the cow jump up and down?" Dad was trying hard for a deadpan look as they pulled out of the carpark.

"I've heard this one so many times, Dad."

"To make a milkshake." He gave the air horn a quick toot.

She groaned and offered him half a mince pie.

"I gain so much weight during school holidays."

Scout ignored him. Dad was the healthiest trucker she knew.

"Only an hour-and-a-half to Eden," he announced. "We'll be there before dusk."

As they passed the turn to Gipsy Point, he checked the side mirrors and frowned at the clouds gathering behind them. "I don't like the look of that weather. Can you re-tune the radio? Let's catch the end of the news."

"Bushfires burning west of Norseman have forced authorities to close a two-hundred mile stretch of highway, isolating Western Australia and causing chaos for Christmas holiday makers. Over a dozen trucks are stranded at Coolgardie with others stopped at Balladonia. In Victoria, a total fire ban remains in force—"

"Gee!" Dad said. "There are fires breaking out everywhere! Jabba does the Melbourne to Perth run. I wonder whether he's been caught up in that." He lifted the microphone. "Breaker, breaker, this is Big Rig north of Mallacoota. Anyone know anything about those truckers stranded in Coolgardie?"

"G'day, Big Rig, this is Bernie in Tar Eater. Hans from Horsham was talking about the Western Australia fires. He reckons one trucker's been stuck there for ten hours and his company's putting on the pressure to keep moving! What's the guy supposed to do—ram the police roadblock?"

"Hey, fellas, Frank in Fizza here. My mate Daz says Christmas travelers are stuck at roadhouses all across the Nullarbor. Temperatures are rising and so are their tempers. Daz heard there's been some—"

Scout sorted her rocks as the truckers swapped stories. Polishing worked best when rocks in the tumbler were a similar size, so she separated them into two piles. As the highway curved north, she hung a t-shirt over the window to block the afternoon sun. She didn't need any more freckles.

"It's soooo hot," she moaned, shifting her legs on the clammy seat. Big Rig's engine was over-heating so Dad had cut the air conditioner. He said she could google the next animal shelter's website, but they were out of mobile range. She stared out the window and before she could complain about being bored, she had an idea—a brilliant one.

"Hey, Dad, you know how there are so many rescue dogs that need forever homes?"

"Mmhmm."

"And you know how truckers are on their own for such long times?"

"Yep."

"Well, I've thought of a plan."

"Why does that not surprise me?"

"I'm serious."

"Okay, hit me with it."

"How about I design a website that matches homeless dogs with truck drivers? I could ask the shelters we've visited to send me photos of dogs that have been in care for a long time. What do you think? We could share their details over the radio, then someone might adopt them. Making a website is easy. And I'd be being a philanthropist donating time instead of money. Do you think that would work?"

"Slow down there, Scout. It's a great idea and I'm proud that you're so caring, but that sounds like a big job."

"It could be a summer holiday project. And even if I only re-home a few dogs, I'd be making a difference. You always say that's better than doing nothing."

"You're right, but let me think about the best way it might work. In the meantime how about I listen to the final innings of the cricket and focus on avoiding impatient holiday drivers?"

While the Hobart Hurricanes thrashed the Sydney Sixers in the Big Bash, Scout took out her notebook and began designing a website. Maybe she could ask Anika to help.

CHAPTER 6
SMOOTHING ROUGH EDGES

"I can see the ocean."

Dad pulled into a holiday park by the beach. He collected their key from the office, then parked Big Rig next to a RV with a side annex. The outside room was made of stripey canvas with zip-down windows.

Scout threw her possum cap onto the bed in the annexe. "Can I sleep out here?"

"No worries."

After helping him unpack, she checked out the trampoline pillow she'd seen near the office. It was wide enough for her bounciest cartwheels. She launched high into the air, then had a sizzling landing.

"Ouch!" The canvas scorched her hands and feet. She rolled off and wriggled her toes back into sandals. She'd come back later when the trampoline was cooler.

In the meantime she checked her emails. There was one from Ms Lawson:

> Dear Scout,
> Thank you for taking part in the Friendship Assignment. I've passed on your messages to Ava and Anika. There were two messages for Sienna. I think you can guess which one I've forwarded.
> Best wishes and Merry Christmas,
> Ms Lawson

Scout lay on the bed with a pillow over her head. Her face burned with shame. What must Ms Lawson think? She took a deep breath and told herself it didn't matter. If her Holiday Plan worked, Dad wouldn't send her back to Arcadia. But she still felt bad. Ms Lawson was nice, in a strict sort of way. Even if she never saw her teacher again, she didn't want Ms Lawson to think she was unkind. Even though her first draft message had been.

She heard Dad's footsteps.

"What are you doing?"

She threw off the pillow. "Umm, it's an experiment. I'm measuring—umm, how quickly my pupils adjust to light and dark."

"Okay." He held up a cooler bag. "I've made a

picnic dinner. Do you want to go to the beach?"

"Yes!"

Anything to take her mind off Ms Lawson and Sienna.

Shallow waves crept over the flat sand. Scout raced into the water.

"Come in and throw me over the breakers."

"Crikey," he groaned, tossing her over a small wave. "You're growing too tall for this game."

After their swim they ate sandwiches by a tide pool. Scout rippled the water with her toes and watched a tiny crab hide. Dad was staring out to sea with a sad expression. She guessed that he was thinking about Mom. Last summer, before Mom died, they'd stayed at a small town north of Eden. She reached out and touched his hand.

"Are you okay?"

He kissed her on the cheek.

On the way back she checked the trampoline. The canvas was the perfect temperature for cartwheels. She bounced with some other kids, seeing who could leap the highest, then jogged back to the van. Dad was watching cricket.

He looked up. "Everything okay?"

"Yep. Who's winning?"

"We are. Brisbane Heat's in trouble. And in other news, so is poor South Australia with record-breaking temperatures. They reckon some inland roads are melting!"

"That's weird!" Scout tried to guess tar's melting point temperature, then said, "I'm glad we're staying near the beach."

"Me too."

She studied the rocks she'd found near Mallacoota. They were dull on the outside but seeing what was inside might be surprising. She filled the barrel of her tumbler to three quarters and measured enough grit to fill the spaces between rocks. Then she poured water over the grit, tightened the two lids, and added a clamp.

Clunk, clunk, clunk.

The sound of tumbling rocks was soothing. They scraped and dipped, smoothing sharp edges to show the beauty inside. She remembered her mean friendship message and wished it was that easy to smooth her own rough edges.

Maybe she should just tell Ms Lawson the truth. Mom always said being honest was best, even when it hurt. She opened Dad's iPad.

Dear Ms Lawson,

I'm sorry about the first message. It was mean and stupid and I never meant to send it. I was deleting it when Dad hit a bump in the road and the message was sent. Thanks for forwarding the other one, though.

I'm trying to be a kinder person, but sometimes I mess up.

Have a happy Christmas,

Scout

Pressing *Send* made her feel a lot better and she sent a silent thank you to Mom. Then she flopped onto the bed with a book from the trailer park library. It was about Old Tom, a famous toothed whale, that once lived off Eden's coast.

Old Tom and other orcas helped whalers by herding baleen whales. In return for their help, the whalers gave the orcas the tongues and lips of the baleen catch. This working friendship was inspired by Yuin locals, the Indigenous people, who hunted baleen whales in the area for over ten-thousand years.

Scout licked her lips and pulled a face, trying to imagine the taste of baleen tongue. She'd seen Old Tom's skeleton at the museum last summer. It was huge. She remembered that day with Mom and Dad.

They'd been so happy. Mom had finished chemo and her hair was growing back curly instead of straight. She seemed to be getting better. Scout sighed. They'd celebrated with dinner at a local restaurant and Mom hadn't even been queasy. It was the best day ever.

Ping. There was a message from Ms Lawson.

Dear Scout,
Thank you for your email.
Please don't worry. I've also sent messages to the wrong person once or twice, and I know that settling into a new school can be hard. Not everyone remembers to be generous.
I've loved having you in my class. Your creativity and ideas are refreshing.
Best wishes and see you next year!
Ms Lawson

Hmm. Maybe she'd see her, and maybe not. Either way, she was glad Ms Lawson wasn't angry. Knowing that her teacher also sent messages by mistake made Scout like her more.

The rocks were still clunking around in the tumbler. It was too soon to see what was inside. Smoothing edges took a long time.

"Hey, Scout," Dad yelled. "Come and look at this, and bring my iPad, please."

There was a weather update on TV.

"After another scorching day, storms have lashed Adelaide's eastern suburbs and residents who'd evacuated from the Cudlee Creek fire were forced to seek shelter from large hailstones. While some of the heavy rain dampened the fire front, huge wind gusts also fanned the flames—"

"Did you see the size of those hailstones," he said. "There's no denying the weather's changing."

Hmm. Scout didn't want to think about that now. "Did they say anything about the fires near here?"

"Not a lot. I'll check the app in a moment."

She opened the book again, but Old Tom's friendship with the whalers made her wonder about the friendship messages.

"Dad, can I use your iPad one more time, pleeease?"

"Five minutes. Max!"

There were three messages. They must have arrived after Ms Lawson's don't-worry email.

The first two, from Sienna and Ava, were brief. One read, "Merry Christmas", the other said, "Happy Holidays"! Scout wasn't surprised they were short. At least they hadn't said, "Hi, Geek-Freak," or "Happy Christmas, Cry-baby."

She deleted them and opened the third email. It was from Anika.

Hello Scout,

Thanks for your message. I was really happy when I saw your name on my list 😃 I don't have a lot in common with some of the other girls.

Your dad's truck looks amazing! I loved watching it tower over the cars as you crept through the after-school traffic. 🚚 Does it have one of those sleeping bunks inside the cabin? I saw a photo of them in a magazine. And if it does, do you get to sleep there?

I've got three positive project things to say about you. The first is that you're smart. And because of you, I know what a geode is 😃 and smashing geodes is fun. The second is your hair. I'd love to have red hair like yours and I reckon those girls who teased you are jealous. The third thing is that you're a bookworm 🐛 Like me. I went to the library yesterday to stock up on science fiction books. They're my favorite. Are you reading anything good at the moment?

Oops, a customer needs help. My parents own a deli. Sorry, I've got to go.

Bye,

Anika

PS Remember how Ms Lawson said that after the first message we can email directly if we want to? I've copied my address and hope you'll write back.

Scout touched her hair and smiled. She started typing a reply then wondered whether she should wait. Was writing back immediately a "normal" thing to do? Would Anika think she was too keen?

She had no idea.

"Two minutes until lights out." Trust Dad! "And it's time to turn off that tumbler."

She tapped quickly.

Dear Anika,
Thanks for your email.
I'm in Eden, on the New South Wales south coast. We're staying at a trailer park and will deliver dog food to an animal shelter in the morning. There's an epic beach and a museum with the skeleton of an orca named Old Tom. It's huge!
I've been reading a book about him. Tomorrow I'll see if I can download some other books. I haven't read much science fiction, but I love science. What's a good one to start with? I get books from the Beechworth Library but we won't be home until Christmas Eve.
Thanks for saying my hair is nice 😃 I do sleep on a

little bunk in the cabin. It's like being in a cubby.
Dad's yelling, "Lights out" so I have to stop. Do you
like dogs? I've attached photos of the puppies I saw at
the Sale Animal Shelter. The tiny one was my favorite.
Want me to send more photos tomorrow?
Good night!

She pressed *Send*, then plumped her pillow. Having a summer pen pal would be fun. And maybe they could be friends when school went back. If she went back. Ms Lawson wasn't just kind and smart; she was brilliant!

CHAPTER 7
TROUBLE IN EDEN

Seagulls skimmed over an ocean dream.

Squawk.

Scout blinked and sat up, wondering where she was. Then she remembered. They were in Eden. And today they'd be meeting more rescue dogs. She checked her watch. How could it be so hot when it was only six?

"Let's have a swim before we leave for the shelter."

"Okay, as long as you can answer this riddle."

"Daaad!"

"What is the strongest creature in the sea?"

"That's easy." She did an eye-roll. "A mussel."

"You're getting way too clever."

"What did the beach say as the tide came in?" she said.

"I don't know this one—"

"Long time, no sea."

He gave her a high-five and went to unpeg their swimsuits from the clothesline. They raced along a sandy track to the beach. Scout pulled on her goggles and followed a school of fingerlings that were darting back and forth below the waves. Dad splashed in after her.

"Let's see who's first to those rocks."

Scout won. Just.

They floated in the shallows, then wandered back to the trailer. After breakfast Scout checked her emails. There was one from Anika.

Hi Scout,
Please send lots more dog photos!
I'm so jealous that you're at a beach. There's nowhere to cool off here and the flies are driving me crazy. Our deli is on the road to that big Christmas craft festival and heaps of people are stopping by for cool drinks and hot pies. I think that's a weird combination. Why not cool drink and a salad or hot pie and coffee? My brother says that's a dumb question.
Mom and Dad don't care what people order, they're just happy to have so much business. Helping with customers isn't fun, but on Boxing Day we're going camping at Lake Eildon. I can't wait!
Now it's my dad who's calling, "Lights out."

I'm looking forward to seeing those doggies.
 Anika

"Dad, can I add Anika to my list of contacts?"

"Is she your friend from school?"

She nodded.

"Okay." He rattled the truck keys. "The shelter will be opening soon. You ready to go?"

She logged off and ran out to Big Rig.

"When's a good time to talk about my idea for the dogs and truckers?" she said. "My pen pal, Anika, might like to help."

Dad stepped up into the cabin. "How about after we've finished this Eden delivery?"

"Great." She checked the website notes she'd already made.

Beep, beep, beep. The Kenworth backed up to the animal shelter gate.

"Hello, Mrs Barker," Dad called. "Where would you like me to put this dog food?"

"In the office would be grand."

Scout helped wheel bags inside, then ran to meet the animals. There were dogs everywhere!

"Wow, full house." Dad looked around.

"Yes." Mrs Barker hobbled into the yard. "We're in the middle of a crisis."

"What's wrong?" Scout stopped to pat a tall greyhound.

"I'm meant to be having hip replacement surgery in Melbourne next week, so I won't be able to look after the dogs. Josie, my assistant, has left for her honeymoon and there's no one else who can help." Mrs Barker looked like she was going to cry. "I don't know what we're going to do."

"There must be someone who can help."

Mrs Barker shrugged. Then she did start crying. Scout remembered Tui's words. "It's okay to cry if you need to."

"Thank you, dear. I've tried everyone. The other volunteers are busy with their families and if I delay my operation I'll go back on the waiting list. Then it might be months until my hip gets done."

"How many dogs are there?" Dad was trying to do a head count.

"Ten. I managed to re-home three pups last week, but then an old collie came in yesterday. His family are doing it tough and can't keep him."

"That's really sad."

"Old Jack needs expensive medicine for a heart problem and their farm's on the brink."

"How about I make a pot of tea?" Dad said. "I'm sure we can think of something." He pointed to the wall calendar and asked Mrs Barker whether she'd heard about the two guys who stole a calendar.

She shook her head. "No."

"They each got six months."

She gave him a weary smile.

While they waited for the kettle to boil, Scout saw an old dog resting in the sun.

"Is that Jack?"

Mrs Barker nodded.

"Can I pat him?"

"Of course." She handed Scout a brush. "If you loosen the grass seeds caught in his coat, he'll be a much happier boy."

Scout combed the gentle collie, then had an idea. "Dad, can I use the CB radio?"

"Yes, but why?"

"I've got a plan."

"What is it?"

"It's a surprise. You'll see."

She wrote down her idea. She shaped it into an announcement then clicked onto UHF 40 and spoke into the microphone. "Breaker, breaker, this is Big Rig in Eden. Calling all truckers in the area. Urgent help needed."

Before she could continue, the two-way radio crackled into life. Messages from nearby truckers tumbled over each other.

"Big Rig, it's Roadrunner six miles from Eden, ready to help. Over."

"Hey buddy, I'm Macka, north of Eden. What's your location?"

"It's Red Thunder. Over. Are you okay, Big Rig?"

"Copy that, Big Rig, Screamin' Banshee is twelve miles out and ready to assist— "

Scout grabbed the microphone. "Wow, thanks everyone, we're okay, repeat Big Rig is okay." She took a deep breath. "This is Scout, Bill's daughter. We're dropping dog food at the animal shelter in Eden and they have a huge problem. Over."

"We're listening, Scout, what's the problem? Over."

"There are ten dogs that need a home for Christmas. Can anyone help? They're desperate. Over."

The airwaves filled with noise as truckers sent Scout's message up and down the line. She ran inside to tell Mrs Barker not to worry. Help was on the way. Dad handed Scout a notebook from his pocket.

"You'd better make a list of all the dogs," he said. "I'll get back out to the rig while you do that and we'll see if anyone calls."

Mrs Barker wiped her tears and helped Scout write the name, breed, and approximate age of each dog.

Jack – Collie about 10 years
Bratwurst – Dachshund 6–7 years
Max, Lulu Bull – terrier pups 8 weeks
Daisy – Kelpie/may have some dingo 7 years
Titan – Staffy/Ridgeback Cross 3 years
Star Princess – Greyhound about 2 years
Meili – Miniature Poodle 12 years
Atlas – Mastiff 2 years
Toby – Tenterfield Terrier about 3 years

Scout ran to the truck with the names. Dad was on the radio, making his own list of callers when Screamin' Banshee pulled into the carpark beside them. A big man jumped down from the cabin.

"G'day, Bill, haven't seen you for a while."

"I'm mostly driving the Hume Highway now. You're looking well, Stan."

Stan patted his belly. "A bit too well, hey!" He smiled at Scout. "Is this your girl?"

Scout held out her hand. "Pleased to meet you, Stan. Thanks for coming to help."

"You're welcome." Stan laughed. "I've got three kids at home and they've been nagging me about getting a dog. Seems like this might be the right time to cave in."

"Come and meet them," Scout said. "They're all friendly. What sort of dog would you like?"

"Well, a young one would be good, but not too young. The missus will skin me alive if I take home a pup that piddles everywhere."

"What about Toby?" She lifted the sweet little terrier into his hairy arms. "He's about three."

Toby licked the trucker's cheek and he grinned. One dog had found a home.

During the morning two more rigs stopped and Scout was so busy that she didn't even think about her Leaving Arcadia Holiday Plan. One trucker took Lulu while another driver fell in love with Daisy. Mrs Barker was thrilled, but there were still seven dogs that needed homes. What else could they do? Scout wondered.

She checked her phone while she waited for an idea. There was another message from Anika.

Hi Scout

I hope you don't think I'm weird for writing again so quickly.

There's no one else I can complain to. 😩 My little brother is so annoying. As if working in the deli and melting in extreme heat isn't bad enough, I have to live with an idiot who thinks arm farts are hilarious.

It's too hot to go for a run, or practice goal kicking, so I'm stuck inside, and with so many tourists in town, the internet is being a snail.

And now we're getting smoke from the bushfires.

Send one of your rescue dogs to save me!

Bye,

Anika

"Let's have some zucchini slice," Mrs Barker suggested before Scout could email Anika back. "A full stomach always helps me think better and there's enough slice for all of us." She opened the small fridge and took a container from behind the worm and flea tablets. "Here it is: my own secret recipe."

CHAPTER 8
MORE HOMES NEEDED

The slice was delicious. As Scout enjoyed the last bite she heard whimpering. Meili the miniature poodle was crouching in her cage. Scout pushed her fingers through the metal bars and let her lick the salty zucchini taste. The poodle spun around in circles and scratched the floor.

"Can I go into the cage and sit with Meili?" she asked.

"Yes, dear, the smoke is making her nervous. I'm sure she'd love some company."

Meili was clever. In half an hour, Scout taught her how to shake paws and how to sit. She was scratching Meili's tummy when a delivery van drove into the yard. A woman put her head out the window. "I heard you need homes for dogs."

"Hello, June," Mrs Barker said. "I haven't seen you for a while and yes—we're desperate."

"I've just finished my last delivery until the New Year. I can't give a dog a forever home, but if it's any help I could mind a couple of animals until early January."

"That would be brilliant." They walked inside and opened the gate to the kennels. "This is Scout," Mrs Barker said. "She and her dad have helped me re-home three dogs today."

"Well done!" June turned back to Mrs Barker. "Are you closing for Christmas?"

"I'm meant to be having an op in Melbourne. Josie's away and seven dogs need homes before I can leave."

"Wow, that's difficult." June patted the dogs. "They're all beautiful, aren't they? This pup should easily find a family, and so will that sweet dachshund, but you might struggle to find places for the big ones. How about I take Titan and Atlas until early January? If anyone wants them as their forever dogs, they can collect them from my place."

"Thanks, June, you're a lifesaver."

Scout crossed the big dogs' names off her list as June led them to her van. They were safe for now.

Only five dogs to go. It was time to get creative.

"Hmm," Scout muttered. "Is there a butcher shop in town?"

"Yes," Mrs Barker said. "It's on the main street."

Scout arranged a little Santa hat on Bratwurst's head and took a photo. Then she used her glitter pens to make a poster.

> Do you love sausages?
> The sweetest sausage dog in town
> needs a home for Christmas.
> Can you help?
> Bratwurst is crossing all his paws,
> hoping to find his new family.
> Please contact the dog shelter
> for more information.

Scout took her poster to the butcher.

"Would it be okay to put this in your window?"

The butcher was happy to help. He even added another line to the poster.

> Five pounds of my best sausages—
> free for Bratwurst's new owner.

By the time Scout returned, Mrs Barker had received two phone calls. Bratwurst was adopted within an hour. Then another family arrived. They'd missed out on Bratwurst, but they took puppy Max instead. Mrs Barker was ecstatic.

"Now there are only three dogs needing homes," she said. "Jack the collie, Star Princess, and little Meili."

Finding a home for Star Princess was going to be a challenge.

"People think greyhounds need lots of space," Mrs Barker said, "but after a few quick zooms they sleep all day." She laughed. "They're snuggly dogs and one of the laziest breeds, but hard to re-home."

The greyhound had been rescued from a racetrack. Although she was gentle with humans, Mrs Barker confessed that she couldn't resist chasing cats.

Scout stroked Star Princess's ears and said, "I'll come back to you." She turned to Meili. The miniature poodle didn't need long walks. She'd be a perfect companion for someone older.

"Is there a seniors' village in town?"

Mrs Barker nodded. "There's one around the corner and another center two blocks away."

Scout combed the fur between Meili's ears into a pretty tuft. She tied it with her own scrunchie then borrowed a matching lead from Mrs Barker.

"Let's go, Meili," she told the tiny poodle. "It's time for you to charm some seniors."

The residents at the first village loved Meili, but no one was able to give her a home. At the second center, a nurse explained that their clients shared one garden.

"They're not allowed to have a pet of their own," she said.

Scout blinked back tears.

"I'm sorry," the nurse continued, "Meili looks like a lovely dog."

Scout led Meili away.

"What will we do with you?" She gave the poodle a hug.

"Wait!"

Someone was shouting. She looked round. The director of the seniors' center was running after her, waving.

"Wait!" She was wiping her forehead. "Goodness it's hot out here—I've had an idea. Does Meili shed fur?"

Scout ruffled Meili's fur. None fell out.

"Perfect," said the director. "I've checked our rule book and a lot of centers now have a therapy dog. They're trained to give affection to people in nursing homes. There's no regulation in our book saying we can't have a dog. Is Meili gentle?"

"Very gentle!" Scout stood up straight.

"Let's try her out."

The director led Meili into the lounge area and introduced her to some of the residents. Their eyes sparkled.

"Oh look—"

"What a sweetheart! See her pretty hairdo?"

"Here, darling, come to me."

Meili went from one resident to the next. She placed her head on laps and licked outstretched hands. An old farmer whistled and yelled for her to circle the sheep. Meili blinked and nudged his leg.

"Good dog," the old man told her. "Good dog."

The director smiled. "Thank you, Scout. We would love to keep Meili. Let's go to the animal shelter and tell Mrs Barker."

Scout was happy and sad. Meili was one of the no-shedder breeds on her wish-list. If she hadn't found a home, Scout was going to ask Dad if they could keep her as a truck-dog. She took a deep breath and remembered the smiling faces of the seniors. Meili had found her perfect place. The poodle would make the residents smile and they'd love her right back.

"Could you send me photos of Meili with her new friends?" Scout said as they reached the animal center. "I'm going to start a scrapbook."

"I'd be happy to." The director smiled.

They walked to the shelter and Scout shouted, "Mrs Barker, we've got some good news."

"That's wonderful!" Mrs Barker hobbled over and hugged her. "You're brilliant."

When Meili's paperwork was organized they waved goodbye to the poodle, then Scout put her hands on her hips. "Back to work."

Two more dogs needed homes and they wouldn't be easy to place. She sent a text to Aunty Sal.

Do you know anyone who wants a rescue dog?

No answer. Sal and Firebird were probably out of range. Scout checked her watch. It was 4 o'clock. Time was running out. What could she do about cat-chasing Star Princess, and Jack, the dog who needed expensive medicine?

She closed her eyes because sometimes that helped her concentrate.

Maybe they could put a donation jar on the counter at the vet surgery. She took out her glitter pens and began a new poster.

Can anyone donate a dollar to help pay for an old dog's medicine at Christmas?

She added Mrs Barker's phone number, then found the address of the town vet.

"Would you drive me to the vet?" she asked Dad.

He was polishing Big Rig's fender.

"It's Saturday afternoon. The vet surgery might be closed."

"Can we try? Please—"

He wiped his hands and fired up the engine. They drove to the other side of town. The vet surgery was open!

Scout showed the receptionist her poster and the jar decorated with Jack's name and a photograph that Mrs Barker had given her. As they waited for the vet to finish treating a guinea pig, she told the receptionist all about Jack, and put five dollars into the old dog's medicine jar.

"We'd love to help," the vet said. "You can leave Jack's jar on the counter and I'll add a note saying that Jack's new owner can buy his medicine at a discount."

"Thank you," Scout beamed.

They drove back to the shelter. Dad had already stacked the dog food, so she helped hose out the last few cages while Mrs Barker fed Jack and Star Princess. She said that if Jack didn't find a family before her operation, he might be able to stay at her house for a week or two.

"He doesn't need exercise and I suppose I could ask a neighbor to feed him," she added.

She closed the office and thanked them for their help.

"We'll stop by in the morning before we leave," Scout promised. "Maybe one of the vet's customers will be in touch by then."

"That would be lovely."

As they climbed into Big Rig, a dusty utility truck raced into the yard, tooting and flashing its lights in the smoky air.

"What—"

The vet receptionist parked and jumped out.

"I'm so glad I caught you," she said. "I've been thinking about your old collie. We live on a hobby farm and I think Jack would love it. Could I meet him?"

Mrs Barker burst into tears.

"Jack's an old farm dog, so that would be perfect." She blew her nose. "Come inside, dear, and I'll introduce you."

It was love at first sight. The receptionist led Jack to her utility truck. He sniffed the wheels, peed on the fender, and smiled the biggest doggy grin in the world as she lifted him into the open tray. Scout took a close-up photo of Jack's happy face and waved as the receptionist and her new best friend drove away.

"What a wonderful day!" Mrs Barker laughed. "I can't believe you've found homes for so many of my dogs."

Scout grinned, but then remembered Star Princess. The greyhound was all alone in the kennel.

CHAPTER 9
STAR PRINCESS

"Wait, Dad! Dogs are pack animals," Scout cried. "They need company. We can't leave Star Princess all alone. She'll fret."

They hurried inside. Mrs Barker's lip quivered as Scout traced the white star shape on the big dog's head. Dad frowned and took his phone into the yard. Scout watched and waited.

When he returned he said, "You know we can't keep Star Princess—" Scout nodded. "But we can be her carers tonight. I've spoken to the owner of the trailer park. He says that as long as Star Princess stays in the annexe, and doesn't come inside the RV, then she can have a sleepover."

"Really?"

"Yes—but just for one night."

Mrs Barker looked so relieved.

"I wish we could do more to help you," Dad said,

"but we have to leave tomorrow. With the catastrophic fire forecast and thick smoke, I'm keen to get through the high country and be on our way home."

"I understand and I'm grateful for all you've done today."

He collected a harness and lead for the greyhound, while Scout ran into the yard to tell Star Princess the good news. She did a few cartwheels on the way.

Star loved riding in Big Rig. It was a short distance to the RV park, so they let her rest her long nose on the window. As her ears flapped in the breeze Star whiffled happily.

At the RV park, Scout folded towels to make a comfy dog bed. She gave the greyhound a snack, then leaned against her trim tummy, rubbing her shell talisman and thinking of Mom.

"We can't keep you, beautiful Star, but I have a feeling that you'll find your forever home soon."

Dad switched on the cricket and whisked up an omelette for dinner, making his usual joke about the Spanish egg farmer saying "O lay" to his hens. Scout pulled her cap over her ears. After they'd eaten, Dad raced Star Princess along the beach while she took photographs. The sun looked eerie in the hazy afternoon sky but it made a great background. And Star Princess won the race easily. She was super-fast.

"I like being a philanthropist," Scout said as they walked back to the trailer.

"Me too, Possum." Dad put his arm round her. "So much so, that I'm going to send one more radio message before the next innings. There must be someone who can give this princess a home."

Scout listened to the crackle of Big Rig's radio as she sent greyhound selfies to Anika.

"Send as many emails and texts as you like," she told her new friend. Anika replied straightaway.

You're so lucky, Scout.

I'd love to have a dog, even just for one night, but I can't. My little brother is allergic to fur!

Tell me about the homes you found for the other dogs.

🐶 Anika

PS I love your cap. Is it a possum?

As they messaged back and forth, Scout hoped they'd be friends at school as well as summer pen pals. If she went back to Arcadia.

She checked the Vic Emergency app. There were alerts across the state, but for now Anika's home at Strathbogie looked safe and so did the area around their little farm near Beechworth. Dad turned up the radio to hear the latest bushfire update.

"December heat records were broken yesterday with Horsham and Hopetoun reaching one hundred and eighteen degrees. Meanwhile in South Australia, eighty-six homes have been lost and the New South Wales bushfires at Bateman's Bay have cut access routes for tourists. The Victorian fire threatening north-east Bairnsdale has been downgraded to watch-and-act, but it's not yet contained. Firefighters also face difficult conditions in deep forest areas along the Great Alpine Road—"

"Poor firies." Dad shook his head.

"I hope those people at the Bairnsdale shelter are okay."

"They'll be following their evacuation plan," he said. "Lucky they'd already found homes for all their animals."

"Are we safe here?" Scout reached over and stroked Star Princess.

Dad gave her a hug. "Don't worry. This smoke is scary, but the fires are a long way from us and my phone's switched to receive alerts for the areas we're traveling through. One more night on the road, then we'll be parked by the river at Sal's. And the night after that we'll be home."

"What if lightning sparks bushfires near our place?"

"Let's not worry about things that haven't happened. Our place is so close to Woolshed Falls, if things turn pear-shaped, we could always go and sit in the water with a wet blanket over our heads!"

Imagining that made Scout laugh.

As Dad listened to the cricket, she downloaded a novel that Anika had recommended. The book was about a flooded city, a good choice for a stinking hot evening. Star Princess rested her nose on Scout's knees as she read the first chapter.

"Strewth, that's a first," Dad shouted from the other room.

"What's happened?"

"The umpires have canceled the cricket! Too much smoke at Manuka Oval. They reckon the Canberra air quality index has just hit hazardous." He gazed at the sleeping greyhound, smiled and changed the subject. "She looks peaceful."

"Did you find anyone who could give Star Princess a home?" Scout crossed her fingers.

"Not yet, but we've done our best for today. I'm going to turn in." He pointed to her phone. "And that's enough screen time for you."

She kissed him goodnight, then gazed out the annex window, hoping to see a falling star so she could make a Christmas wish for the greyhound. Tomorrow she'd get back to work on the Escaping Arcadia Holiday Plan.

Hours later she woke from a nightmare. Aunty Sal was surrounded by fire and calling for help. Scout sat up, shuddering, then she heard a low growl.

"What's wrong?"

Star's nose was pushed against the zipped door of the annex. Scout could see her fur bristling.

"Who's there?" Dad yelled.

"Is that you, Bill? It's me, Theo from Red Racer."

Scout hopped out of bed and held Star's collar as Dad stepped out into the moonlight.

"Sorry about the late night visit," Theo apologized. "I wouldn't normally bother you after ten, but my freight has to be in Wollongong tomorrow morning."

"No worries. Is everything okay?"

"Right as rain, mate, besides all this darn smoke. I'm here about the greyhound."

"Star Princess?"

"That's a mouthful of a name!"

"Yeah." Dad laughed. "We've been calling her Star." He flicked on the lights. "Come in. This is my daughter Scout, and that's Star."

Theo held out his hand for Star to sniff. She wagged her tail.

"Gee, she's tall. My grandfather was in the racing game when I was a kid and I often felt sorry for the doggies." Theo frowned. "Some owners treated their animals badly. When I heard Big Sal's message, I thought I could give something back to at least one greyhound."

Scout cheered. "Will Star ride in the truck with you?"

"She sure will. I reckon Star will be great company on overnight drives." Theo tapped his leg and Star curled against him.

"Looks like we're going to be mates," he said.

Scout gave Star Princess one last cuddle, then Theo lifted her into the cabin. He gave them a thumbs-up, and fired up Red Racer's engine. Scout watched the truck's tail-lights fade into the darkness. Everyone needed a safe forever home. She tried not to feel too sad.

After an early morning swim, they drove to the shelter to share the good news with Mrs Barker, and to leave Theo's adoption money.

"You really are my Christmas angels," Mrs Barker said. "And, Scout, I'd like you to have this."

She held out a box. Scout peeped inside and gasped. "Thank you, Mrs Barker!"

She'd always wanted a charm bracelet. Maybe this could be her special piece of jewelry, like Tui's greenstone.

"That's very generous," Dad said, "but your bracelet looks precious. I don't think we can accept it."

Mrs Barker squeezed his arm. "It is precious," she whispered. "The bracelet was my sister's, but she's passed on now and neither of us had children. Please let Scout take it. She loves animals and look, there's a kitten and a mouse charm."

Scout stroked the silver animals and turned to Dad.

"Are you sure?" he said to Mrs Barker.

"Perfectly." She fastened the bracelet around Scout's wrist. A Sydney Harbor Bridge hung between the kitten and the mouse. There was also a lucky horseshoe charm, ballet shoes, and an orca. Scout hugged her.

"I'll think of you whenever I wear it," she said.

"That would make me happy."

"Good luck with your operation," Dad added.

"Thank you. I'm all packed and, thanks to you two, there's plenty of time for me to drive to Melbourne. With road closures and that Bairnsdale fire, I might have to go the long way via Cooma."

Scout jingled her charms. "I'll send you photos from the rest of our trip."

"Thank you, dear, that would be lovely."

As Mrs Barker waved goodbye, Dad said, "The drive to Batlow's about five hours. If we leave now, there should be time to stop along the way at the Yarrangobilly Caves."

"Have I been there?"

"Not since you were very little."

They passed the sign to the whale museum and he slowed down. "Do you want to see Old Tom's skeleton again before we head into the hills?"

Scout squeezed the scallop shell in her pocket and shook her head. She'd rather hold on to the memory of them being there as a family of three.

"Let's keep going," she said. "The air might not be as smoky in the mountains."

"Alright." He changed gears and accelerated.

CHAPTER 10
HIGH COUNTRY

Scout held the bracelet close to the dashboard photo as Big Rig rumbled out of Eden, wondering which charm Mum would have liked best. Then she stretched out her fingers, trying to picture Mum's hands. She remembered how soft they'd been and the way they smelt of coconut moisturiser. She wiped away a tear and turned to Dad. "How long to the Yarrangobilly Caves?"

"About three and a half hours, but we'll need to drop a pallet at Adaminaby. The town is an hour before the caves."

They followed the highway north, then traveled along a pretty forest road toward Bemboka. Scout started composing arguments to convince Dad that she didn't belong at Arcadia.

"Right," he said suddenly. "Let's hear about this amazing website idea. Was it something about matching homeless dogs with truckers?"

"Yes!" She thought for a moment. "Hundreds of dogs need homes and there must be hundreds of truck drivers who would love to have a truck-dog. All they need is someone to bring them together. Like we did with Theo and Star Princess."

"And who might that someone be?"

"Me, of course. Making a website's easy. If I keep it simple and list ten dogs at a time, drivers will be able to scan through it quickly. We know lots of carers now, so finding dogs won't be a problem. Then we could tell truckers about it on the UHF channel."

"That sounds like a lot of work. How would you keep it going when you're back at school?"

"Once it's online, I could update it once a month or in the next school holidays. That wouldn't take long and even if we only find one dog a home it'll be worth it."

"We?"

Scout laughed. "Okay, me. Or maybe me and Anika."

"Your pen pal?"

"I haven't asked her yet, but I think she'd like to help. Her brother's driving her crazy."

Dad tapped the steering wheel. "It would be nice to find homes for dogs like that heeler Tui was trying to place—"

"Fly could be top of the list."

"You're a shrewd one, my little philanthropist. Okay, you have my permission, and let's hope old Fly finds his forever home."

"Can I use your iPad to send an email to Tui?"

"Go for it."

She asked Tui if it was okay to include Fly and Archie the old spaniel on the website. Then she emailed Anika.

Hi Anika,
I've thought of something that might help homeless dogs.

I'm going to start a website that matches shelter dogs with truckers. There'll be photos of truck-friendly dogs like the old spaniel and blue heeler from Sale. And information about each dog's personality and what they like to do. Would you like to help? Once they find homes we could add new dogs. How great would that be?

Are you good at designing websites?

At the moment we're on the Snowy Mountains Highway, heading for Adaminaby. Dad reckons the town has a big statue of a trout!

Bye for now.

She shut down the iPad and sketched some ideas for a home page banner.

"Dad, do you think those two big dogs from Eden would be truck-dogs?"

"The staffy cross could probably get into a cab."

"Okay, I'll include Titan, and I've also got Fly and Archie from Sale. What about one of the Sale puppies?"

"Kelpies are top-notch at jumping and they're smart. I reckon those pups would grow into great truck-dogs."

"Yesss." Scout punched the air. "That's six. How about Nellie, the big gentle dog at the first shelter?"

"Yep, she'd be good, and the older terrier that had all the pups. What was her name?"

"Dotty! I'll email Tony and ask if she and Ginger are still at his shelter."

She sent messages and wrote draft biographies for the Sale and Eden dogs. Then she opened the Lost Dog Haven website to remind herself of Ginger's details.

"Hey guess what," she cried. "Freckles and Speckles have a banner through their photo. It says they're on trial in a new home."

Dad tooted the air horn. "You beauty!"

"I've got nine dogs on the list so far. I think we'd need one more."

"There might be a truck-kind-of-dog in Adaminaby."

"Okay, I'll wait till we visit them before I look for others."

The Adaminaby dogs were all in foster care so Dad dropped their supplies and they went to take selfies in front of the Big Trout. Scout made tuna sandwiches in the cabin and they ate them outside on the grass by the giant fish.

"Let's see who can do the best trout pout," Dad suggested.

He perfected his until she agreed that he was the winner.

"You're too good," she said.

"Really? I'm not usually good at fishing for compliments. All I get are snags."

"Let's make today joke-free."

They drove to the Yarrangobilly Caves where a guide led them underground along a magical pathway past glittering stalactites and stalagmites. Scout felt like a storybook character as she blew cloud puffs into the chilly air.

"These caves were formed around four hundred and forty million years ago," the guide explained, "and the stalactites and stalagmites have taken thousands of years to develop." She shone her torch onto the largest formation. "This stalagmite has probably averaged four inches every thousand years."

Scout did a quick calculation.

"It's at least twenty-eight thousand years old," she whispered.

The guide raised her eyebrows. "Possibly," she said.

The mind-boggling numbers made Scout's heart soar. She took dozens of photos to send to Anika. The cave setting was more fantasy than science fiction, but she hoped her pen pal would like them anyway.

When they stepped back into the sunlight she blinked.

"It's too hot to swim in the thermal pools," Dad said, "but let's have a quick look at them before we go."

Scout stared at the steaming water, imagining twenty-six thousand gallons of natural spring gushing through rocks every hour.

"I love this place!"

Dad laughed. "Being here with you as an eleven-year-old, instead of as a three-year-old, adds a whole new dimension."

He ruffled her hair, and as they walked back to the truck, she wondered whether this was a good time to mention leaving Arcadia. She kicked a pebble. Dad looked so relaxed. Perhaps it was better to wait.

Big Rig grumbled up the steep Snowy Mountains Highway toward Batlow. They pulled into a wayside before dusk and Dad got busy at the microwave.

"What's for dinner?" Scout peered round him to see what he was making.

"My pasta surprise."

She smiled and arranged camping chairs beside a picnic table. "Can I plug my tumbler into the solar battery? The rocks need another hour before I can check them."

"No worries. The battery should be fully charged."

They enjoyed a high-country sunset and slurped pasta as Scout searched the darkening sky for her favorite constellation.

"There it is—the saucepan!"

"Did you hear about the restaurant on the moon?" said Dad.

She shook her head. So much for the joke-free day!

"Great food, but no atmosphere."

"Far out." She bit her lip, trying not to grin as she went to check her tumbler.

The rocks had been polished on and off for twelve hours now. Tumbling often took longer but she was impatient to see if any showed promise. She unplugged the tumbler and unscrewed the lids. Then she tipped the grit onto a sheet and checked her treasures.

"Any good ones?" Dad looked over her shoulder.

Scout held up her favorite. "This stone might be okay after more tumbling."

He had a closer look. "Hmm, interesting. And now, how about I make some hot chocolate?"

"Yum."

She packed away her tumbler and put the polished rocks into a bag. Dad passed down two steaming mugs and the marshmallows bobbed against Scout's nose as she drank.

"Look!"

A shooting star crossed the sky.

She imagined Theo and Star Princess sitting in a wayside near Wollongong, watching the same star.

"It's been a good day," she whispered, stroking her scallop shell.

"It sure has," Dad agreed. "And if Santa's been watching, I reckon you're definitely on the big fella's 'nice' list."

"I hope so!"

She imagined a sleigh full of presents and sucked the pink marshmallow she was saving for last.

CHAPTER 11
JAI AND THE PUGGLE

"What's going on?" Scout jumped down from her bunk and peered through the windscreen. Thick smog blanketed Big Rig. "Have the fires changed direction? Are we safe?"

"It's okay. I've just checked the bushfire app. There are no outbreaks nearby and the wind hasn't changed direction. Those East Gippsland fires are still moving south, away from us."

"Then why's it so smoky?"

"The fire has grown overnight. Don't worry. As soon as we've dropped food at the next shelter we'll head out of the forest."

The Batlow animal shelter was surrounded by bushland. It wasn't far from their overnight parking bay. Scout had called ahead, so a teenager with dreadlocks was waiting to help Dad lift bags onto a trolley. He adjusted his *Sea Shepherd* cap, shook

Dad's hand and said, "Hi, I'm Jai. Thanks so much for all this food."

"No worries. This is my daughter, Scout."

"Hi," Scout said, blushing as she smoothed her crinkled shorts. Jai looked just like Ned, the lead singer of the Lamingtons boy band. She stared at the floor to hide her flaming cheeks.

Jai said he was caring for birds, joeys, and possums rescued from beside the highway. There was also Rusty, a red heeler that someone had left on their doorstep.

"She's smart," Jai told them, "and luckily she doesn't chase the other animals."

Scout took a photo of the heeler. She could put Rusty on the website next to Fly. With two lovely heelers available, truckers could choose their favorite color.

As they unloaded supplies, Dad explained that this shelter needed bandages for birds and animals that had been hit by traffic. "If you look behind the pallets," he pointed, "there are smaller boxes at the back."

Scout jumped inside Big Rig and pushed the boxes along to him. She also grabbed a bag of dog food for Rusty.

"Thanks," Jai said. "If the wind turns, I'm worried we'll get embers from those Gippsland fires and if that happens we'll need all these bandages for burnt wildlife."

"Let's hope not." Dad looked grim.

"They reckon the flames are so big that they're making their own weather. Weird, hey!" Jai frowned. "If lightning sparks a fire here, there aren't enough of us to defend a mega-blaze." He pushed a loose dreadlock into his cap. "Luckily we have emergency carers for the animals in case things get worse."

Scout looked at the map and said, "Gippsland is a long way from here—" Then she blushed again. What a dumb thing to say. As if he didn't know that.

"It is." Jai scanned the hills. "Our worst nightmare would be a bushfire getting into those steep wilderness areas and burning north. The undergrowth is tinder-dry. That type of fire would be hard to contain."

"Let's hope it won't come to that," Dad said, "and that you and the animals stay safe." He closed Big Rig's back door. "You're probably busy, so we won't stay long."

"There's plenty to do, but I've got half an hour. Do you want to meet the animals before you go?"

Scout stared at her dad with puppy eyes. "Can we, please?"

"Okay, but no longer than thirty minutes."

Jai lifted a box onto the table. He reached in and showed Scout the tiny creature curled under a warm towel.

"This is Missy. She's a puggle, a baby echidna. Bushwalkers found her mother by a scorched log last week. The mom was too weak to save, but when we checked her pouch we found Missy."

"You poor little thing—"

"Would you like to hold her?"

Scout sighed as the puggle snuggled against her skin. "She's so soft."

"Her quills are beginning to harden." Jai pointed to an adult echidna in the yard. "Soon they'll be as strong as that one's."

He squeezed droplets of a special milk formula over Missy's snout and her strange tongue flicked about, searching for it.

"I've changed my mind," Scout whispered. "Now I want to be a wildlife carer, instead of a photographer."

"You could be both," Dad said.

"That would be cool." Jai grinned.

Scout imagined days of feeding puggles and wombats with Jai, then taking cute photos of them. And him. She sighed again.

"We rescue injured birds too." Jai showed her a huge bird cage. As they stepped inside he moved slowly toward a wary owl.

"This one's a boobook. His wing's broken, so he needs to rest. In a few weeks he should be strong enough to release." He lifted up a couple of squawking chicks. "And these cheeky magpies are growing stronger every day."

"We have magpies at home," Scout told him. "Their chicks sound like human babies."

"I know. It's weird, but good—right?"

"Exactly! I'm making a scrapbook of birds and animals that we've met at different animal shelters." She was trying not to stare at his amazing eyebrows. "I wonder, would you send me pictures of the puggle as it grows?" Her cheeks flushed again. She sounded like a six-year-old.

"That sounds fun." He nodded. "I've kept a scrapbook of all the injured animals that I've helped. Adding new photos is the best thing."

Scout beamed and gave him her email address.

"Thanks again," he said, shaking their hands.

Her skin tingled.

They passed the statue of a Batlow apple as they drove through town. It was almost as big as Adaminaby's trout. Scout's phone pinged when Big Rig came in and out of phone range. Maybe it was Jai sending photos. There wasn't enough signal to download messages. She tapped her foot, wishing for better range.

"Yum, cherries!" She pointed to a roadside stall. "Can we buy some?"

They pulled over, bought a bag, and she challenged Dad to a pit-spitting contest. "Best of three."

"Good to see that fancy boarding school hasn't changed you!"

She remembered her Holiday Plan. "If I lived at home, we could do fun things like this all the time."

Dad laughed and shook his head.

After an impressive six foot spit, Scout won the contest, then they continued driving. While Dad listened to his whodunit, she refreshed her messages. There was nothing from Jai, but there was one from Anika. She sucked a cherry pit and read it.

> Hi Scout,
> I definitely want to help you help the homeless dogs and I LOVE making websites. Brilliant Idea: When the dogs find homes, we could post good news stories about them, like that big greyhound and your dad's friend.
> What colors do you think would be good for the banner? I like red, but it's your choice. Send me some plans and I'll get started tonight.
> Are you still in the Snowy Mountains?
> I can't wait till we close the deli for Christmas. I'm trying to finish my book (I'm up to a really scary bit), but customers keep asking me where things are!

Send more animal photos.
Bye,
Anika

Scout chose her best puggle picture and pressed *Send*. Anika replied immediately.

Wow, that's so cute.
What is it?
PS: I can lend you my book if I ever get to the end.

"Another message from Anika?" Dad adjusted the air vents.

"I've sent her a puggle photo and she wants to know what it is. I guess it doesn't look much like an echidna yet—"

Hi Anika,
It's a baby echidna. Bushwalkers found her injured mother. The mom didn't make it, but Missy was safe in her pouch. And guess what? The carer at the Batlow shelter looked like Ned from the Lamingtons. His real name was Jai and he had exactly the same eyebrows!

Jai says the puggle is about five weeks old. I'd love to keep it as a pet, but they're protected so I can't. And they need special food. Once this puggle's well enough,

Jai will set it free.

I'm so glad you want to help with the website. Red's a good choice. It's got the lowest vibration frequency, but helps people take action. And that's what we need. Adding good news stories is a brilliant idea 😃

We're heading to Wagga Wagga now and then onto Wodonga. We'll be home at our block tomorrow night—Christmas Eve!

And I'd love to borrow your book. Scary stories are great.

What are you hoping to get for Christmas?

See you, Scout

They stopped at a historic pub in Tumblong for lunch.

"Only another hour till Wagga," Dad said. "We're making good time. How about a short detour via Gundagai to see another dog?"

"The one on the tucker box—didn't we go there when I was little?"

"Can you remember that? You were only three."

"There's a photo of us standing in front of it."

Dad laughed and sang, "Where the dog sits oooon the tuckerbox, nine miles from Gundagai—"

Fifteen minutes later Big Rig turned into a busy carpark. There were tourists everywhere.

"Where's the dog?"

"There." Dad pointed.

"It's tiny. I remember it being much bigger!"

"That's what happens when you grow up."

Then they stopped in Gundagai to print Scout's animal photos and to buy a scrapbook. The book came with sheets of different colored backgrounds and stickers with words and pictures to add to each page. Scout couldn't wait to get started. She roughed out a plan for the first page.

Shadows were lengthening by the time they reached Wagga and Dad parked in Aunty Sal's backyard by the Murrumbidgee River. Sal was on the road, but she'd left a note on the shed door.

Homemade chicken pie in the fridge. Key in the usual place. Help yourself to tomatoes if any are ripe.

See you Christmas Eve at the Barnawatha Sundowner. Love Sal

xxx

"Yum," Scout said. "Aunty Sal's chicken pie is the best."

While Dad checked the rig's oil and water, Scout began her scrapbook. She chose an orange background for the cover page and drew a map of Victoria and southern New South Wales onto it. Then she used the stick-on letters to write "Operation Dog Food" as a title. On the first page she added stickers of city buildings, then glued on a selfie of herself and Dad standing in front of their truck at the Frankston Pier.

On the next page, she pasted a collage of Sale animal photos, arranging the dogs in the middle, then adding rabbits and the tabby cat along each side. She remembered the warm smell of the tiniest pup and sighed. She'd give anything to have a dog of her own.

"Okay," Dad wiped his hands, "Big Rig is tuned and ready to roll. Let's make dinner before the cricket starts."

Sal's vegie garden was huge. Scout picked two ripe tomatoes, some rocket, and a cucumber while Dad warmed Sal's chicken pie. Then they sat under a huge river gum and wolfed into the food.

Scout remembered other family picnics by the Murrumbidgee with Mom, Dad, and Aunty Sal. When they were together Mom loved teasing the rest of them about how much they looked alike.

"Three orange peas in a pod," she used to say.

"Oi, only gingers are allowed to make red-head jokes," Sal warned, but everyone knew she loved

Mom's teasing. Those memories of them all sitting by the river gave Scout a warm, loved feeling. She couldn't wait to see Aunty Sal at the Barnawatha barbecue tomorrow.

CHAPTER 12
WEBSITE PLANNING

Scout woke to magpie calls. Their detailed warble patterns made her smile. She picked some of Sal's strawberries to put on her cereal, then Dad said she could check emails. There was a reply from Anika.

> Hi Scout,
> I'd love to have a puggle too. And send me a photo of Jai.
> My brother and I got new clothes and presents for Diwali so I'm not expecting much for Christmas. But more books would be good!
> Does your dad ever deliver to the mountains? Mom says that if you're driving anywhere near the Strathbogie Ranges, you should stop by for a meal. We're on the main road and there's plenty of space to park a truck. And Mom is a good cook.

I could ask if it's okay for you to have a sleepover
when we get back from camping.
If you want to.
And if your mom and dad let you.
My little brother's being nosy and trying to read this,
so I'm going to annoy him and stop writing. You are
SO lucky you don't have a brother!
I'll add more when he's gone,
 Anika

Scout swallowed. She'd have to tell Anika about Mom. But how?

Dear Anika,
I forgot to tell you.
I didn't tell anyone at school, but—
You probably didn't know,

She deleted those lines and took a deep breath.

It's just me and Dad now. Mom died last June.
A sleepover would be fun. I'll ask if I can.
Scout

She took a deep breath and pressed *Send*. Oops, she'd forgotten to attach a photo of Jai. She chose one of him smiling as he held the puggle, added a quick caption, then pressed *Send* again.

"Hey, Possum, are you ready to go?"

"Yep—and, Dad, Anika asked me if I want to go to her place in January for a sleepover."

"That sounds fun. Where does your friend live?"

Was it too soon to call Anika a friend? She hoped not.

"Near Strathbogie. Her parents own a deli. She said to stop by if we're ever passing through."

Dad laughed. "That's not on my usual route, but please thank her." He checked his watch. "And in the meantime, we'd better get going."

They left Sal's place and the GPS directed them to Wagga Wagga Pet Rescue. On the way, she re-read Anika's message and asked Dad what Diwali was.

"I think it's some kind of lights festival. Why?"

"Anika said she celebrates it."

"Sounds like fun."

She switched on a Christmas playlist.

"Do you have any more jokes for me?" He cocked an ear in her direction.

She thought for a moment. He was looking for any chance to start up the Dad-jokes again.

"What does going to the movies have in common with a Christmas tree?"

He waited.

"They both have stars."

"That's a sparkly one!"

Wagga's rescue center had two lively boxer dogs and lots and lots of cats.

"Are we even carrying cat food?" Scout shrugged.

"No, the philanthropist's a dog lover, but if the cats are hungry enough I reckon they won't mind." Scout wasn't so sure. Most of the cats she'd met were pretty fussy.

The boxers were too bouncy to be truck-dogs, but she didn't mind. She already had nine profiles and there might be a truck-kind-of-dog at the last shelter in Wodonga. She bent over to throw a stick and giggled when one boxer licked her sweaty forehead. Then the other one licked her arm.

"That tickles!" The more she giggled, the more they licked.

"Look out," the carer warned, "boxers have enormous tongues."

"Really?"

"Supposedly the world's longest dog tongue belonged to a boxer."

"How long?" Estimates raced through Scout's mind. As long as the width of the rig's steering wheel? No, too big. The length of her notebook? Maybe. Or her foot, which was almost eight inches long?

"I don't know. I just remember reading that somewhere."

She couldn't wait to check it out.

The carer led the boxer dogs into their cage, so the cats could have a turn in the garden. A feline climbing frame criss-crossed the yard. Scout watched kittens chase each other through carpet tunnels, and tap pretend mice dangling on strings. The older tabbies were content to lounge in the sun.

"That's a beaut cat maze," Dad said when he'd finished stacking the dog food.

"One of our volunteers made it. The cats love climbing through the frame, and there's a section we can close to keep the birds and lizards safe when we're not with them."

"Win-win!" Dad laughed, then he turned to Scout. "We'd better get moving."

"Where are you going next?" The carer walked outside with them.

"Wodonga. It's our last drop-off."

"Thanks so much for the food."

"I hope the cats'll eat it."

"Don't worry, it won't be wasted. We normally have a lot of dogs, but most were adopted for Christmas. Fingers crossed they're not all returned next week."

"Goodbye, bouncy boxers." Scout blew them two kisses and climbed into the rig.

"Homeward stretch." Dad sighed as they drove south toward Wodonga. He flicked his playlist until "Driving Home for Christmas" came on, and then sang along in a pretend-crooning voice. Scout covered her ears.

The highway was busy. Holiday-makers with RVs and boats joined them in the slow lane, while smaller cars whizzed past. Scout held her breath as drivers cut in front of them.

"Idiots!" Dad said through his teeth. "I wish they understood how long it takes me to stop. Driving's already difficult enough with all this smoke." He shook his head. "Only one more drop to go."

While he focused on the road, Scout googled record-breaking dog tongues and found that Brandy, a boxer from Michigan, had a seventeen-inch tongue. What? That was the size of the steering wheel! She sent the link to Anika, then researched Diwali.

"Hey, Dad, you were right. Diwali is a Hindu festival celebrating the triumph of light over darkness. People light candles to celebrate."

"Hopefully not on total fire ban days."

"No—it was at the end of October."

The Olympic Highway joined the Hume and once they passed the odd-shaped Ettamogah Pub, Scout knew Albury–Wodonga wasn't much further. She sketched a plan for the website's home page: red with lots of yellow paw prints and a green truck that looked a lot like Big Rig. What should they call it? She pushed back her cap and wrote down a few ideas:

Dogs and Truckers

Matchmaking Dogs and Truckers

Trucker and Dog Matchmaking

Truck-Dogs

She couldn't decide. Maybe Anika would have another brilliant idea.

Dad turned up the radio for a bushfire update.

"Almost one thousand homes have now been lost in New South Wales. Major roads are closed across the state and motorists are urged to check updates. Police ask all drivers to use their headlights."

Scout looked at the shadowy cars passing them. "Why don't those drivers turn on their lights?"

"Beats me."

"In other news, astonishing stories of heroism are emerging from the Adelaide hills where one brave firefighter has rescued at least six koalas and taken them to safety. Amazing scenes are also appearing across social media of desperate koalas drinking from water bottles. Meanwhile other animals are finding relief wherever they can. One family has photographed a large kangaroo cooling off in their backyard swimming pool—"

"Imagine that." Dad thumped the steering wheel. "Poor animals, they must be terrified. The Bushfire App tells *us* which way to go to safety, but they must be confused by all this smoke."

"If we had a swimming pool, animals could drink from it." Scout imagined treading water as wombats and wallabies gathered around her.

"Too many chemicals. And we have Woolshed Falls."

Scout nodded. The Falls were better than a pool, but that sparked an idea. "We could become wildlife carers."

"One thing at a time, young Scout. Let's complete this mission before taking on anything else."

"They'll be needing carers."

"They will—and I'm happy to talk about the idea after Christmas. Looking after injured wildlife is a huge job. Your mom had a few joeys once and she was up half the night feeding them. Their milk formula costs a fortune." He smiled. "But it was worth it all when the roos were strong enough to hop free."

Scout gazed out the window, imagining a houseful of joeys, possums, and koalas.

Dad pointed to a sign on the highway. "Welcome to Victoria," he read as they rumbled across the Murray River.

CHAPTER 13
MEETING MOLLY

Big Rig eased through the Wodonga Christmas traffic and they parked in a quiet street not far from the animal shelter. Dad loaded the last pallet of dog food onto the forklift and delivered it to the doorstep.

"Hooroo, Mrs Jellicle!" He knocked on the door.

"Hello, Bill, thank you. My hubby will be along soon to help stack the bags." She put down a little pug and turned to Scout. "You must be Bill's daughter."

Scout nodded and held out her hand for the pug to sniff.

"I need to collect our Christmas ham and groceries," Dad said. "Would it be all right if Scout stays here for half an hour? I have to pick up something secret as well." He winked at Scout.

"Mr Puggles and I would love the company."

Scout grinned and waved the pug's paw. Mrs Jellicle left her with the dog while she went to sort her paperwork.

"Sit," Scout ordered. Mr Puggles stared at her. "Sit!" She tried again.

He flopped onto the floor.

Maybe it was worth trying again with treats. Then the phone rang and Mrs Jellicle answered. "Hello, Wodonga Animal Shelter—"

Scout knew that eavesdropping was rude, but in a small office she couldn't help it.

"Oh no, not another one," Mrs Jellicle groaned. "That's dreadful."

Then there were just random words: "emergency puppy farm, RSPCA, damaged hips—"

"Of course you can bring her here. I'll ring the vet now."

"What's wrong?" Scout said as Mrs Jellicle hung up.

"RSPCA officers have just closed a backyard puppy farm."

"Someone on the south coast told me about them."

"This place sounds particularly cruel. The owners kept mothers in cages with barely enough room to turn, having litter after litter of pups." Mrs Jellicle sighed. "They've given most of the animals to the Australian Terrier Society, but one mother's hips are so badly damaged, the officers say she needs to be euthanised."

"What does that mean?"

Mrs Jellicle hesitated. "The vet will give her an injection and put her to sleep."

"But that's not fair! Someone might want her."

"She can't walk." Mrs Jellicle squeezed Scout's hand. "It's the kindest thing to do."

"I saw a dog once with a little cart and wheels stuck onto its hips."

"I've seen that too." Mrs Jellicle patted her shoulder. "And occasionally dogs can be healed with rest and massage, but those carts are expensive. The money for one could pay for months of food for other homeless dogs."

"But—"

The phone rang again. It was Dad. He'd been delayed and asked if Scout could stay there another 20 minutes. Mrs Jellicle said that was fine. Mr Puggles had fallen asleep so Scout worked on her scrapbook. She'd finished the Ninety Mile Beach page and was arranging photographs of Eden when an officer arrived with a small Australian terrier.

The dog's golden-red fur was matted. Her breath was terrible and her skin smelt musty. Despite all this, and her broken hips, the terrier lifted her head and licked Scout's hand.

"Can I hold her?" said Scout.

Mrs Jellicle draped a blanket over her lap and the officer carefully lowered the dog onto it.

Scout cradled the terrier. "You're so beautiful," she whispered. "Surely someone could look after you. I'd love to."

The dog looked deep into her eyes and seemed to understand. As it licked her nose, she remembered Mom's words: a pet is for life.

Scout chewed her lip. Mom also said that taking time to choose the right pet was important. This injured dog wasn't on Scout's wish-list, but she'd trade a litter of poodles to help the terrier.

"Do you know the dog's name?" Mrs Jellicle asked the officer.

"The sign on her cage said Molly."

Scout gasped. Her mom's name!

"Are you all right?"

She nodded. Molly wasn't the dog she'd imagined, but if they didn't help her, Molly would be euthanised. That didn't seem right. Scout was rushing in. She knew that wasn't good, but she also knew she couldn't let this dog die. She touched the shell in her pocket. Mom said that she would know when she found the right dog. And right now, she knew.

But how could she convince Dad? She stroked Molly's ears and wished she could ask Mom for advice. She closed her eyes to focus.

The phone rang again.

"The vet's delivering a calf," Mrs Jellicle told the RSPCA officer, "so she's running late."

Good. That would give Scout more time.

"We can look after Molly until the vet arrives," Mrs Jellicle said. "If you need to go."

"That would be great." The officer looked as if a weight had been lifted. "It's been a busy day."

As the terrier snuggled against Scout, she practiced what to say to Dad.

- Molly is gentle.
- She doesn't need exercise and could watch the world pass by from a truck window.
- This terrier would be a perfect truck-dog.

She asked Mrs Jellicle how much a dog wheel cart might cost.

"Even second-hand pet wheelchairs cost over a hundred dollars."

When Dad arrived back, Scout took a deep breath.

"Dad, I need to talk to you. It's important."

"Is everything all right?"

"No." She handed Molly to Mrs Jellicle and led him outside. "A mother dog's come in with broken hips. They don't think she'll be able to walk again, and so the vet is coming to euthanise her, but with proper care, she might be able to walk. And even if she doesn't, she still deserves love after everything she's been through."

"Slow down," he said.

"There's something special about her, Dad, and Mrs Jellicle says that maybe she could be fitted with one of those doggie wheelchair things—"

He stepped inside and looked at Molly. "Is this the dog?"

"Yes, and her name's Molly."

"Really? Like Mom?" He stared at the frightened terrier. "Poor girl. What's happened to you?"

Mrs Jellicle explained about the puppy farm.

"I'm sorry for her," he said, "but, Scout, this isn't practical—"

The phone interrupted him.

"The vet's on her way," Mrs Jellicle told them.

Scout gripped her father's hand.

"Please, Dad, it's almost Christmas. You know Mom and I were making a list of dogs we might get. This Molly isn't the dog we planned for, but she wouldn't need long walks and she's used to small places. She could be a truck-dog like Star Princess and I could help out during the holidays . . ."

He frowned.

"Please. We could give her a fresh start and I'll save all my pocket money for a little wheelchair if that's what she needs."

Dad looked at the dog and then back at Scout.

When the vet arrived she checked Molly's hips, ears, teeth, and skin.

"Can she be saved?" Dad seemed to have been won over.

Scout held her breath as the vet hesitated.

"Molly's ears are clogged. She has dental disease and a nasty skin rash on her belly. That can all be treated, but Molly's hips are badly damaged. She may never be able to walk normally. Or perhaps not even walk at all."

Scout winced. "Would it be very expensive to fix her teeth, ears, and skin?"

The vet sat beside her.

"I could clean her teeth and ears and I wouldn't charge you a fee for that, but she'll still need creams for her skin and antibiotics for her teeth. Even at a discount, her medicine might cost hundreds of dollars. With the hips, an operation would be too exhausting for her at the moment. We could give her anti-inflammatory tablets, keep her calm for six weeks and see whether she's able to walk, or if she's strong enough for reconstructive surgery."

"If we go ahead could I pay the bill over a few months?" Dad said.

"Of course."

He turned to Scout. "Are you sure this is the right dog for us?"

She nodded. "I know she is."

He ruffled Molly's coat. "Okay," he said, turning to the vet. "Please do what you can for her."

The vet smiled and said, "I'll take Molly back to my surgery for a bath, teeth, and ear cleaning. She'll be ready to collect in a couple of hours."

As they left, Mrs Jellicle gave Scout $50.

"To help with Molly's medicine," she said.

Scout hugged her.

While the vet was treating Molly, Scout had an idea. She found two jars in Big Rig and asked Dad if she could use her pocket money to buy a jumbo bag of lollies.

"That won't be good for your teeth."

"They're not for me," she said. "I've got a plan."

"Another one?"

They walked to a deli and she bought a huge bag of lollies. She popped one caramel into her mouth and offered another one to Dad. Then she used the rest to fill one jar, counting each lolly as it went in. There were eighty-eight.

She made a sign and glued it onto the second jar.

> How many lollies are in the jar?
>
> $2 for one guess
>
> $5 for three guesses
>
> All money goes toward medicine for our rescue dog, Molly.

She showed her dad the jars. "We can raise money for Molly at the Christmas Eve sundowner."

He kissed her forehead. "Where do all your brilliant ideas come from?"

CHAPTER 14
TRUCKER BBQ

Molly's ears were spotless. The grime and fleas were washed away. Even her teeth sparkled. Scout scrambled up the steps into Big Rig and helped Dad lift her onto the front bench. Using an old blanket, she'd made a snug bed for the terrier between them. She stroked Molly's back until the dog settled.

"Thanks, Dad," she whispered.

He winked. "How could I say no to you and another Molly?"

Scout thought she would explode with happiness. The drive to Barnawatha, Dad's home depot, would take only twenty minutes, and Molly was a good traveler.

"Looks like you'll be a perfect truck-dog," he said, reaching across to scratch her clean ears.

Scout saw the truckers gathered in a paddock just off the Hume Highway. Dozens of rigs were parked on the grass. As Big Rig joined them, she waved to Theo and Star Princess. Then she saw Sal.

"We've got a surprise!" she yelled from the window.

"Remember the vet's instructions." Dad's voice was soft and slow. "Too much excitement isn't good for Molly. We need to make sure she stays calm."

"Okay."

Scout climbed down and ran to hug her aunt.

"Hello." Sal kissed her cheeks. "I've missed you. What's your surprise?"

"We've got a dog!"

"Really?"

"She's a rescue terrier and her name's Molly."

"Wow! She's come to the right home."

"Dad says we need to keep her calm. She's resting in Big Rig."

"Are the windows down?"

Scout nodded. "You can meet her if you like." She told her aunty about Molly's history and her damaged hips.

"Those puppy farmers are mongrels," Sal growled.

They climbed into the cabin and Sal held out her hand for Molly to sniff.

"Don't you worry, beautiful girl," she whispered. "You're safe now."

She stroked Molly's ears and tucked a rug around her poor little hips, then they walked back to the barbecue. Scout put the lolly jar, money jar, and a number-guessing sheet on a table beside the salads.

"What's this, young Scout?" Theo picked it up.

Truckers gathered as Scout explained about Molly's past and how they'd rescued her from euthanasia. "We're saving money for her medicine, and maybe even a walking wheelchair."

"Good for you."

Before long the jar was filled with $10 notes and $20 notes. The truckers were paying a lot more than $2 for a guess. Scout wasn't surprised. Truck drivers were like one big family. They always helped each other out.

"Now what's this about you growing taller than me?" Sal stood beside her.

"I reckon I'm close—"

"Back to back." Sal was rounding her up like a sheepdog.

Scout laughed as they stood, bottom to bottom.

"There's not much in it." Dad held his hand over the top of their heads.

"But I've still got the edge," Sal said, butting Scout with her bum.

"Not for long."

Scout munched watermelon and listened to her aunt's news while Dad shared jokes with Theo.

"Have you heard this one?" he said. "When the traffic cop told me to stop impersonating a flamingo, I had to put my foot down—"

Theo wasn't going to be beaten. "Did I tell you that I went onto the Weight Watchers website?"

"No—"

"It said I have to disable cookies!"

"Brilliant."

They laughed and nudged each other, then Dad said, "Scout told me a new one about—"

Before he could finish, Scout licked watermelon juice off her hands, then went to check the guessing chart. It was full. A trucker's name was written in every space. She counted the money in the jar. Over three-hundred dollars! More than enough for Molly's skin creams and medicine.

She tapped her glass with a fork to get people's attention.

"Wow, thanks everyone. We have three-hundred and thirty-six dollars to help Molly and now it's time to announce the lolly jar winner."

She checked all the guesses. Some truckers were way off, but Jillo from Pink Lady was spot-on.

"There are eighty-eight lollies in the jar," she shouted, "and the winner is—Jillo!"

The drivers cheered. One jumped into his truck

to blare his horn as Jillo high-fived Scout. Then the drivers settled down and went back to sharing stories about near misses and idiot holiday drivers. Some talked about the bushfire-devastated areas they'd seen on the way to the barbecue.

"I'd love to meet Molly," Jillo whispered when the cheering had stopped.

"Come on." Scout led her over to Big Rig and they climbed into the cabin.

"What a sweetie. Maybe I should get a rescue dog to keep me company on the road."

"So many dogs need forever homes," Scout told her. "My friend and I are making a website with animals from some of the shelters. What type of dog would you like? We're adding biographies for ten dogs that would suit a trucking life."

"I don't care about breeds, but a gentle one like Molly would be nice."

"There's a quiet terrier called Dotty at a shelter near Frankston. She's had too many pups. Or there's another dog, Nellie. She's lovely, but a bit anxious."

"They both sound good."

Scout showed her the photos. "I can send you our list with these photos and all the details when I get home tonight."

"That'd be great, Scout."

Jillo held out a card with her email address and as they walked back to the barbecue they heard Aunty Sal's voice.

"Sausages are ready!"

Sal loaded meat, salad, and crunchy bread onto Scout's plate.

"There's a surprise for you on the front seat of Firebird, Scout. I think we're close enough to Christmas for you to open it after dinner, if you want."

Scout hugged her aunty. Sal gave the best presents. The surprise could be anything!

She took her plate and sat beside Theo and Star Princess. Between bites, she snapped selfies with her greyhound buddy wearing a Santa hat. She sent the best one to Anika.

There was pavlova and strawberries for dessert. Scout finished her last bite then ran to Firebird. She climbed into the cabin and saw a parcel wrapped in a Save the Ringtail Possum t-shirt. Aunty Sal reckoned wrapping paper was wasteful, so the strange packaging was completely normal.

She untied the ribbon and cheered. It was the vegie-powered battery kit she'd been saving for. Scout couldn't wait to get home and see which vegetables generated the most power. She suspected potatoes, because of their starch, but she wasn't completely sure.

As shadows lengthened across the paddocks, Jillo shared her lollies with the other drivers. Sal raised her mug, making a toast to road safety and old mates who were no longer driving. Then it was time to pack up.

Dad lifted Molly onto the grass so she could pee before they drove the final eighteen miles to their farm near Woolshed Falls. Scout had loved their philanthropic road trip, but now it was time to go back to their farm. She hoped their first Christmas without Mom would be okay.

Dad hummed carols while they waited to cross the busy highway and Scout wondered which dog would be right for Jillo. Maybe Dotty—

The road to Beechworth was quiet. As Big Rig left the forest, her phone pinged. It was a message from Anika.

Hi Scout,
I'm so sorry about your mom. I don't know what to say. I wish I'd known.
We've closed the shop—at last 😃 and Mom is cooking gulab jamun, my favorite dessert. Yuuum!
And guess what else? Mom said that after we get back from camping, you can come for a sleepover.

If you want to.
And if your dad says it's okay.
Mom's happy to collect you from Beechworth.
I hope you'll be able to.
Merry Christmas. I'm really glad we're friends. If you don't hear from me in the next few days, it's because we're out of range.
Xx Anika

PS Jai is gorgeous!!!

"Yesss!" Scout cried. So many good things had happened today. And tomorrow was Christmas.

Dear Anika,
I'm glad we're friends too.
I googled Diwali and it sounds like fun.
BIG NEWS – We've got a dog!
She's a rescue terrier with damaged hips from having too many pups, but if she rests for a few weeks, we hope she'll be okay. I can't wait to tell you about her, but we're almost home. More soon and I'll send a photo after this.
Her name's Molly.
xx Scout

She took a quick photo and pressed *Send* as they turned off the main road and drove onto a smaller track. After a couple of miles, Dad pulled over and she jumped out to open their gate.

"Home at last!" she told Molly. "I hope you'll like it here."

She latched the gate, did a double cartwheel and raced Big Rig to the house. Then she helped carry Molly inside and left the exhausted terrier alone to smell her new home and settle in. While Dad hosed the rig down, she filled each of their wildlife water bowls. Thirsty birds flew down immediately, but she knew the lizards would wait till she was gone.

When Dad finally came inside they lit a candle by a photograph of Mom. The Christmas tree was in its usual place near the pot-belly fireplace and Dad had decorated it the way Mom always did. Scout tucked the present she'd made for him under the tree, then looked around. Last year's family Christmas photo was in pride of place on the mantelpiece beside their old nativity scene. She rearranged a fallen shepherd and blinked back tears as Dad eased into his favorite chair with a cool beer.

"Merry Christmas," he said. "There's something big under the tree for tomorrow, so maybe you'd like to open this small one now."

He took a present out of his pocket and handed it to her. She read the card: "For my little philanthropist, with love from Dad, Mom, and all the homeless dogs." She untied the pretty ribbon, opened the box, and took out a silver charm. It was a dog and it even looked a bit like Molly. He must have bought it in Wodonga. She clipped it onto her bracelet next to the lucky horseshoe. Then she lifted Molly onto Dad's lap and took a new family selfie to put beside the old one.

"Happy Christmas," she whispered. Molly licked her hand and a warm feeling spread across Scout's tummy. Perhaps everything was going to be okay.

She opened her summer playlist and added "Feliz Navidad." They sang quietly together, then Dad held her hands and danced her around the room, just as Mom would have done. Molly wagged her tail and woofed.

Later, when Scout lay on her bed, she reached under her pillow and wrote "Molly" across the top of her dog wish-list. She sighed and looked around her room. It felt good to be home.

CHAPTER 15
CHRISTMAS

"Happy Christmas!"

Scout hoped Dad would like the bookmark she'd made. It was green, his favorite color, and made of felt with a small gemstone dangle. She'd polished the stone in her tumbler and put the bookmark into a book about the world's best cricketers.

"Howzat!" Dad shouted. "I saw this book in a shop window and thought it looked good. And what a great bookmark."

"I made the felt from some old wool."

"You're the cleverest daughter I have."

"The only daughter!"

He grinned. "I'll treasure it, thank you." He took a closer look at the dangle. "What type of stone is this?"

"Jasper. There's a card in there with its qualities."

"Jasper is a spirit stone of courage and wisdom," he read. "It's known as a nurture stone because it helps bring tranquillity in times of stress. Jasper has strong earth energy and helps neutralize environmental pollution. Gee!" He grinned. "That should sort me out."

"I don't know if all that's true."

"It can't hurt, though." He gave her a hug. "Thanks, Possum, I love it. Here's my present to you."

He pointed to an enormous box under the tree. Scout knew that didn't mean the present would be big. He was such a joker—always loved packing presents in layers of paper or boxes as a trick. Sure enough, as she unwrapped layer after layer, as if it was a game of pass-the-parcel, he could hardly contain his laughter.

And at last—the final box!

"Oh wow," she cried as she opened it. "My own laptop! Thank you, Dad. That's fantastic."

"You're welcome. And now you can stop borrowing my iPad."

"I can use it to edit the Dogs and Truckers website."

"And for your school projects—"

"Definitely. This is the kind everyone at Arcadia uses. It's perfect!"

"Well, that's a relief. The guy in the shop said it was a good model, but I guess he would."

She peeled off the plastic covering and slid in the battery.

"There's one more thing," he said, holding out an envelope. "Your mom wanted me to give you this letter on Christmas morning." Scout held her breath as she recognized her mother's handwriting. "She wrote it the week before she died."

"Do you know what it says?"

He shook his head. "I'll grab some veggies while you have a read."

She traced her name on the envelope. The handwriting was wobblier than Mom's usual writing. She'd been frail that last week. Scout sat by the Christmas tree. She held her scallop shell and took out the letter.

My Dearest Scout,

Merry Christmas, little possum. I'm so very sorry that I wasn't able to win my battle and be with you today. This first Christmas will be sad, but if you can be a little bit happy as well, that's what I'm hoping for as I write.

How's Dad doing? He wears his tough guy, funny mask, but being strong is hard work. Be patient with him.

Now, about our dog plans. It's been such fun researching different breeds together. Even though there won't be a pup for your birthday

> this year, one day the right dog will appear.
> You'll know in your heart when that happens.
> I wonder what kind it will be.

She reached across to scratch Molly's soft tummy and whispered, "I wish Mom could have met you." Molly shuffled closer and licked Scout's toes as she continued reading.

> I hope school is going okay. Your dad and I spoke about Arcadia being the best option for now, even though boarding school will be different from what you're used to. You've probably made new friends by now, but even if you haven't, I'd love you to give Arcadia a year's trial.
>
> In the end it's your decision. Dad and I agreed that'd be fair. But if you go back to our local school he'll have to find another job. We both know how much he loves Big Rig, so if boarding school does work, that'll be great, but if it isn't right for you, that'll be okay too. More than anything we want you to be happy.
>
> My beautiful girl, I'm so proud of you and heartbroken that I can't be there for you anymore. I know you'll be okay. You're strong and generous and so clever with your Maths and

Science. Who'd have thought you'd turn out logical like me, when you look so much like your dad?

Ill always be with you, Scout, in your heart and in the rocks and leaves and shells that we loved collecting.

I love you xx Mom.

Scout wiped away her tears and put the letter in her pocket, keeping it close so she could read it again later. Mom's words were like a warm hug from far away. When Dad came back with a basket of zucchini, carrot, and silverbeet, he whispered, "You okay?"

She nodded and started to set the kitchen table with Christmas napkins and bonbons. She gathered a few leaves from Mom's favorite tree and arranged them in the middle. Aunty Sal was driving over to join them for lunch and it was too smoky to eat out on the veranda. She filled a jug with rainwater, lemon, and lots of ice. It was going to be a scorcher.

While Dad made stuffing for the chicken, she washed carrots and potatoes.

"I know you're not happy at boarding school," he said suddenly, "but for now, I think it's the best option."

She didn't know what to say. Her Leaving Arcadia Holiday Plan was a disaster.

Dad put the dinner in the oven to roast, kissed her forehead, then settled down in his favorite chair. Molly lay by his feet as he worked on a crossword and Scout sighed as she opened Aunty Sal's present to read the instructions once again.

The vegetable energy generating kit included a second box with everything she needed to make a potato-powered clock. Did she want to make a clock, or experiment with different vegetables to see which kind generated more power?

"Eeny, meeny, miny, moe."

Molly's tail wagged as Scout tapped both boxes. The clock won.

She arranged everything on the floor. There was a digital clockface with wires, tape, a copper coin, zinc strips, galvanized nails, alligator clips, and two big potatoes, which she knew held phosphoric acid. The instructions had pictures of each step. She laid newspaper across the floor, then cut a slit into the end of each potato. She pushed copper wire in each slit, then put one nail into the end of each potato. Juice oozed onto the newspaper.

She looked at the instructions again. "So far, so good."

The picture showed how to use the alligator clips to connect wire from Potato One to the clock's positive terminal and then connect the nail from Potato Two to the negative terminal. The last step was to connect the wire from Potato Two to Potato One.

She crossed her fingers and looked at the clock. The second hand was moving. It worked! Her potatoes were powering the clock.

"Dad, come and look at this."

Molly wagged her tail and dragged herself across the floor as well.

"Your aunty is going to love that," he said.

They heard Sal's car long before she opened the gate. Firebird was Sal's workhorse, a big Kenworth like theirs, but her absolute pride and joy was Hattie, her 1969 HT Monaro. Hattie was burnt orange with black GT stripes on the doors and bonnet. Her refurbished engine sounded lethal.

"Merry Christmas." Sal flung off her hat and stepped in front of the fan. "Whoa—it's a furnace out there! These eighty-five plus days are slaying me. And now that wind has picked up again."

"Not what the firefighters need at the moment."

"You're not wrong, Bill." Sal stroked Molly's ears then plonked a small cooler on the kitchen bench. "Here's the plum pudding and custard."

Scout licked her lips. "I love your custard."

Sal ruffled her hair, cranked up the music, and sang "White Christmas" as she spun Scout around the room.

"What do Santa's elves listen to while they get the presents ready?" she asked Dad.

"Too easy, Sal. Rap music, of course."

Scout groaned, wondering who was the worst joke-teller in the family. "Come and see my potato-powered clock."

"Wow, that's impressive! Let's do the other experiment after lunch."

They set out a potato, a carrot, an apple, a tomato, and a lemon.

"Which one do you think will generate most energy?" said Sal.

"The potato, because it has so much starch."

"I think so too, and thinking about that is making me hungry."

"Lunch is ready." Dad stirred gravy while Sal carved. They wore silly hats, pulled bonbons, and raised their glasses to both Mollys.

"Yum," Scout said as Dad poured gravy over her chicken.

Sal took a bite then raised her glass again. "Thanks, Bill. You're a culinary legend."

"This is so much better than boarding school food," Scout murmured, trying to revive her tattered Holiday Plan as she *accidentally* dropped some chicken near Molly's nose.

She noticed Dad and Aunty Sal exchange a glance. Was he deliberately missing the point?

Then he puffed out his chest. "Not just a culinary legend, a green-thumb as well. Everything in this salad is from our garden." He tossed the lettuce, snap peas, and cherry tomatoes.

"And modest!" Scout took another bite of her drumstick.

"How's Molly settling in?" Aunty Sal winked as another sliver of chicken fell from Scout's hand.

"Great."

"Stop feeding her at the table." Dad tried to look stern, then he held up a juicy triangle of meat. "Who wants the parson's nose?"

Sal shook her head. "The chicken bum is all yours."

Scout laughed, scraped her plate clean, and held it out for seconds.

"Do you mind if we watch the news between courses?" Sal said. "I've volunteered to help if any fires break out in the Upper Murray."

"Go for it." Dad was helping himself to more of his carrots.

"Volunteers across several states have given up their Christmas Day to work alongside firefighters, back-burning and rescuing burnt stock and wildlife."

"You and the other volunteers are total legends," Dad said as they watched terrifying scenes on the screen. Scout shivered as huge flames devoured their beautiful forests.

"Weary firefighters will build containment lines today and tomorrow before more hot weather is expected on the weekend. At this koala hospital in New South Wales, carers are looking after more than seventy injured animals today."

"Poor things," Scout whispered. "I wish I could do something to help."

Sal stood up. "Your mom taught you to sew, didn't she?"

"Yes." Scout touched the letter in her pocket. "But I'm not very good."

"That doesn't matter. Wildlife carers need pouches for injured kangaroos. I've already made half a dozen.

The pattern's easy."

"Could we start one now?"

"Sure can. Where are your mom's boxes of fabric?"

"In the shed."

"Right, let's find some soft material and set you up on the sewing machine while your dad whips the cream and warms up the pudding."

Sal downloaded two patterns, then helped Scout thread the machine. One drawstring pattern was for joey pouches, and another smaller one was for wrapping bats with singed wings.

"I'll text you the mailing address once I'm home tomorrow."

"Dessert's ready!"

Sal's pudding was delicious and Scout drowned her piece in custard. After lunch, as the adults dozed, she read Mom's letter again, feeling warm inside. Then she experimented with her vegetable energy kit, amazed that lemons gave the most power. She checked her results, then read the booklet that came with the kit. It was because lemons are most acidic. When Sal woke she wanted to see the results so Scout tested the fruit and vegetables a second time.

"That's amazing," Sal said.

Before she left, she helped Scout sew two flannelette joey pouches. Doing something practical took Scout's mind off the suffering animals. She hugged her aunt goodbye, then held them out to admire her handiwork.

"I hope you'll help save a burnt kangaroo."

CHAPTER 16
NEW FRIENDS AND OLD FRIENDS

Scout made blueberry pancakes for breakfast, then they soaked the veggie garden before Dad settled down in front of the TV.

"Ahh, Boxing Day sport." It didn't take much to make Dad happy. He held a cold drink holder against his face for a moment. "Yacht racing after lunch and cricket all day. The ground's packed and the Test's about to start. Do you want to watch the toss?"

The cricket umpire threw the coin and the New Zealand captain chose to bowl. The crowd roared, but Scout wasn't that interested.

"I'm going to sew wraps for bats," she said.

"Okay, and hey, Scout—"

"Yep?"

"Can you think of anything more amazing than a talking bat?"

She thought for a moment. The answer was probably

something to do with a creature. "A spelling bee?"

"Too clever." Dad went back to his happy place.

"Hey, Dad—"

"Mmhmm."

"What do you get when you cross a vampire with a computer?"

"Neck ache?"

"No, love at first byte." Dad looked puzzled, so she spelled it out. "B.Y.T.E., get it?"

"Way too clever!"

The bat wrap pattern looked straightforward enough. As Scout searched through Mom's fabric she found material that she remembered from old shirts and dresses. Memories sat with her as she sewed. Then she wondered what Anika was doing on her camping trip. Hopefully lots of swimming. Between wraps, she sent her an update on Molly.

> Dear Anika,
> Happy Boxing Day.
> You're probably out of range, but I wanted to email anyway. How's Lake Eildon? I wish I was there swimming with you. It's over ninety-five degrees here!

Did you like the photo of Molly? I've taken heaps more. She's been sleeping a lot, but Dad says that's to be expected. Molly came from a puppy farm where people kept her in a cage. She wasn't allowed out much and being cramped for so long messed up her hips. That's why she can't walk, but I hope she'll be able to one day.

Dad says we've got to let her rest, and be patient. She's lying next to me while I write, wagging her tail every time I stop to pat her.

Besides cuddling Molly, I've been sewing pouches for injured joeys and making wraps for bats. I hate seeing all the burnt animals on TV. Can you sew? Want me to send you the patterns?

I've attached a photo of the bat wrap I've just made. How good is the spooky material? It's leftover from some leggings Mom made when I was little.

Have fun camping,

xx Scout

She took the wraps to show Dad.

"That's great," he said. "Where will you send them?"

"Aunty Sal's got a mailing address."

They ate leftovers, then Dad nodded at their Christmas tree. "What looks like half a Christmas tree?"

"Dad, you say this every year, and Christmas was

yesterday."

"Then what's the answer?"

"The other half," she thought for a moment. "How about this one? What happened to the dad who was addicted to Boxing Day sandwiches?"

"What?"

"He had to go cold turkey."

"Love it. We could start thinking up New Year jokes soon."

"Or not!"

He grinned and flicked channels to watch the Sydney to Hobart yacht race. The boats were jostling for a starting position and their tall sails looked spectacular against the blue sky. As the gun fired they raced toward Sydney Heads.

"Can I ride down to Woolshed Falls for a swim?" Scout said.

"Sure, maybe Sam would like to join you."

"Probably already there."

Months had passed since she'd heard from her old bestie. When she first went to Arcadia they'd spoken on the phone a few times, but it felt weird. Sam wasn't chatty and nor was she. Although they'd hung out together since they were little, they'd mostly ridden their bikes, climbed trees, and done experiments. Talking on a phone didn't really work for them.

"Are you okay to go on your own?"

"I'm eleven and a half, Dad, and it's a seven-minute ride!"

"Nine minutes uphill on the way back—"

"I'll be fine."

"Take your phone in case I need to call."

"Because of the fires?"

"Because I'm your dad and I like checking in."

"Okay."

She pulled on her swimsuit, and possum cap.

"Don't forget your hat."

"It's on my head!"

The Falls car park was full. Scout locked her bike and climbed down the rocks to where her old school mates would be. Halfway down, she stopped, feeling shy.

Sam saw her and waved. "Hey, Scout, you're back!"

"I am."

"With the same possum cap!"

She laughed.

"Jump in here," Sam said, "and I'll show you where a big yabby is hiding."

Scout dumped her towel and pulled on goggles. Sam didn't ask her about school or anything, which was great.

They dropped bits of apple near the yabby for a while, watching it lunge, then they joined the others on a shady rock. Some of the girls wanted to know what Arcadia was like.

"It's okay, I guess. Not as good as here."

And then everyone went back to talking about Christmas and who was going to the local berry festival. Scout helped Sam eat the rest of his snacks, they listened to music, swam, and did nothing much at all. It was perfect.

After a couple of hours, the two of them rode back. Scout was dripping with sweat by the time they reached her gate.

"See you!" Sam waved and disappeared into the smoke haze.

"Bye."

Why couldn't people at Arcadia be this easygoing? Scout pedaled up the driveway. Then she remembered Anika, who seemed a lot like Sam, and the other girls at her geode party who had been okay until Sienna messed things up. She rode harder. Maybe she hadn't given Arcadia a fair go. The science labs were awesome and so was the library. Arcadia had hundreds more books than her old school. If she'd had a friend, it mightn't have been too bad.

"*Comanche* is still in the lead," Dad said as she flopped

onto the couch, "but not by much. How was the water?"

"Fresh, but after riding back, I'm hot again."

"They reckon we'll get to one hundred and four degrees tomorrow."

"I wish we could camp at Woolshed Falls."

"Wouldn't that be good? Are you hungry? I cut up some rockmelon. It's in the fridge."

"Yum." Scout wiped juice from her chin as she checked her messages. There was one from Jai!

Hey, Scout,
Hope you made it home safely.

Here are some photos of the animals. They haven't changed much since last week, but the puggle's stronger now.

We're doing okay, with carers ready to mind animals if those fires come any closer.
Stay safe, Jai

She traced Jai's name and wrote it on a piece of paper next to her own. Then she printed the photos and went to find her scrapbook. The pages up to Eden looked great. She left space to add a section for Adaminaby and Yarrangobilly, then chose a forest background for Batlow. There were so many cute puggle pictures. She decided to make a double page of them.

As she spread stickers and photographs across the kitchen table, she sang along to her favorite song by the Lamingtons.

"I like this one best," she told Molly, holding up a picture of the puggle licking milk. Molly snuffled at her hand and wagged her tail.

When the Batlow pages were done she sent a photo to Jai and asked him if it was okay to include Rusty

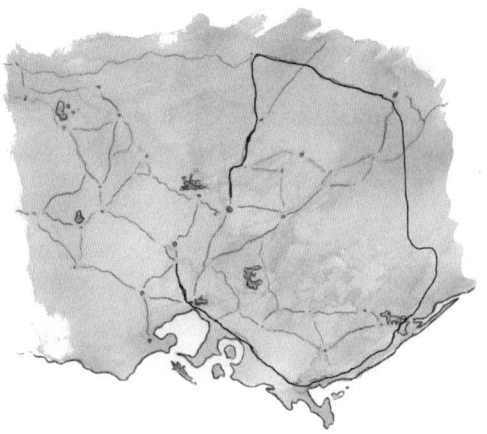

on the matchmaking website. Then she turned back to the cover page of her scrapbook and drew a red line on the map, marking all the places they'd visited.

If they drove back to Arcadia at the end of the holidays, the line would make a strange-shaped travel circle. She frowned. If . . .

Maybe tonight was a good time to talk seriously to Dad about letting her stay home next year? But then she remembered the words in her mother's letter:

> I'd love you to give Arcadia a year's trial. In the end it's your decision. Dad and I agreed that'd be fair. But if you go back to our local school he'll have to find another job.

She stroked the Ninety Mile Beach shell in her pocket. Why was learning to be good so hard?

"You ready for dinner, Scout?"

"Yes." She sighed. Dad had loved his lazy Boxing Day. She didn't want to spoil that with an argument about school. Her tummy rumbled. "So ready!"

CHAPTER 17
TRUCKER AND DOG MATCHMAKING

Scout twirled the charms on her bracelet, wondering how Mrs Barker was doing with her hip. She chose some photos and started an email to tell her about Molly.

> Dear Mrs Barker,
> I hope your operation went well.
> We're home now and there are no bushfires near us, but the air is full of ash.
> After Eden we visited animal shelters in Adaminaby, Batlow, Wagga, and Wodonga. And guess what?
> There was a dog called Molly at the last shelter. Her coat was matted and her ears were clogged, but worst of all, her hips were damaged from being in a puppy farm cage. I guess you know how painful bad hips can be.
> Molly needed a forever home or else she was going to be euthanised.
> So we've adopted her!

She's at home with us now and we're hoping that one day she'll be able to walk again. I've attached a photo. Isn't she lovely?
Thanks again for giving me your beautiful bracelet. The charms are tinkling as I write and there's a new one. Dad gave me a silver dog charm for Christmas. It looks just like Molly.
How are Meili and Jack? Do they like their new homes? My friend and I are making a matchmaking website. We're trying to re-home rescue dogs with truckers. Here's the link. It's not live yet, but I've attached a screenshot of the way it'll look. I've included Titan. Is that okay?
I'll update the site before the next holidays, so if you have any new animals that would make good truck-dogs, please send their details.
Dad says hi and we hope you'll feel better soon.
Best wishes,
Scout

There was still no email from Anika, but Scout sent her a quick message anyway.

Hi Anika,
I hope you're nowhere near the bushfires.
We can't see past the end of the driveway here and

everything's covered in ash. Dad's put towels around all the windows and doors, but smoke still gets in.

My aunty is a volunteer fire-fighter. She's on standby in case the fires come closer.

I hope they don't.

See you, Scout

PS Jai messaged me!

In the morning, she helped Dad water the garden. They wore masks to protect their throat and lungs, but Scout's kept slipping.

"Perfect weather for staying inside and watching the second day of the test," Dad said. "What are you going to do today, Possum?"

"More scrapbooking. Once I've finished the Wagga page, I'll add photos of Molly and Wodonga, then finish with a Barnawatha page."

"Sounds good."

She showed Molly the photo of Star Princess that she'd taken at the barbecue.

"You were too sick to meet Star," she whispered. "She's another rescue dog. One day you guys might meet on the road."

"Are you talking to me?" Dad said.

"No, I'm telling Molly about Star Princess."

"Okay."

"And best of all," Scout continued, stroking Molly's ears, "you both have a new home."

Molly's feathery tail thumped the floor as Scout read the front page of her scrapbook, "Operation Dog Food", and said, "Who would have thought our philanthropy journey would lead us to you?"

During the cricket lunch break Dad made toasted sandwiches and they listened to the news.

"December 17th was Australia's hottest day on record, but that statistic could be beaten this weekend. With temperatures expected to rise, firefighters fear that gusty winds and dry lightning strikes will spark more fires.

And in sport, *Comanche* has snatched the lead in the Sydney to Hobart yacht race as the supermaxis enter Bass Strait—"

Her phone pinged. She gobbled down the last bite and excused herself from the table.

Hi Scout,
We're back.
At last!
You know how I was looking forward to swimming and sunbaking and reading? Well, none of that was fun in thick smoke, and my brother Pran has asthma, so we've come home early.

All of our doors and windows are closed, but like you said, the smoke still gets in. Mom and Dad have put Pran's puffers all around the house, but he's mostly staying in bed watching movies.

What's happening with the website? Is it live? I can't wait to match dogs with truckers.

Do you want to come for a sleepover when the fires are out? Mom says she can drive to Beechworth to collect you.

 Anika

PS I've read all my books!

She emailed straight back.

Hi Anika,

I'm glad you're home. Sleeping over would be fun. I'll ask Dad.

The website's almost ready. Here are the log-in details. Can you check there aren't any mistakes?

Let's go live today and maybe we can make a match before the year ends.

x Scout

PS I'm sorry about Pran. Hope he'll be okay.

She skipped into the kitchen.

"We're going live!"

Dad looked confused.

"The website, 'Trucker and Dog Matchmaking'."

"Ahaa. Fun name. So you've finished designing everything?"

She nodded.

"Make sure all replies come via me."

"Yes, Dad!"

"And have the animal centers said it's okay to include their dogs?"

"Most have. Mrs Barker sent a message saying Titan can be included and Jai gave an okay for Rusty." She didn't mention that Jai's message was disappointingly short (he was probably busy with bushfire prep). "Tony from Frankston said Nellie and Ginger would love to go online. I haven't heard from Tui, but I've listed Fly, Archie and the pups. I hope she'll answer soon."

"Sounds like you're all organized," Dad said.

"Anika's double-checking for typos and her mom says it's okay for me to go to her place for a sleepover once the bushfires are out."

"Do you want to?"

"I want to spend time with Anika." She scuffed her toe on the floor. "But I don't want to go there for a sleepover. I've missed being home—"

Dad scratched his head. "Why don't you ask Anika to come here? They sound like a nice family and I'd rather meet Anika's parents before leaving precious cargo in the wilds of Strathbogie."

"Thanks Dad, that'd be great."

Molly barked as someone knocked at the door.

"Hey, Scout, it's me, Sam. Want to go for a swim?"

She turned to Dad. "Is that okay?"

He checked the Bushfire App and nodded. "But come back in an hour."

Woolshed Falls was super-crowded. They searched for yabbies, paddled, and lazed on the rocks. She didn't want to leave, but knew Dad would worry if she was late.

"I'm back," she yelled, hanging her towel on the veranda.

"Thanks for being home on time."

He high-fived her as she went to check for messages. Anika had replied, saying the website was ready to go. She read through it one more time.

TRUCKER AND DOG MATCHMAKING

Breaker, breaker!

Hey, Truckers, would you like a friend to take on the road? Our website matches truck-friendly dogs with drivers. The dogs below are looking for someone to love. They're at different animal shelters across Victoria and New South Wales, but if the dog you love is not on your truck run, our network can help bring your new best friend to you. Available dogs will be updated regularly. Please contact the shelters listed or send a message to Bill:
BigRig@Barnawatha.com

NELLIE:

Gentle Nellie would love having her ears stroked between gear changes. She's a mixed breed girl who enjoys chasing balls. Nellie is looking for someone calm to help her feel safe. Are you the trucker for her? She's waiting near Frankston, Vic.

TITAN:

There's no need to lock your rig at the station when Titan's on board. This boofy guy looks tough, but he's really a big softy. Titan's favorite thing is cuddles. You can meet this gentle giant in Eden, New South Wales.

DOTTY:

Dotty is small enough to fit in any truck cabin. Or even in a toolbox. She's a gentle girl who's had many pups and now needs 'you-and-me-time' while she sees the world. Available for adoption in Frankston, Vic.

FLY:

If you're looking for a true-blue friend, you'll love this guy. He's playful and smart, and Fly is dreaming of escaping his cage in Sale. Please come and save him.

RUSTY:

Want a loyal friend to blend in on those dusty inland roads? Then Rusty is your girl. She's about three years old and her carer says she's very smart. Rusty is at an animal refuge in Batlow. She's kind and gentle. Could she be your special truck-dog?

TRIPLE TROUBLE:

These three kelpie pups are smart and cute. You can choose a name and, with training, your new buddy could help herd stock into a truck. These scallywags are in Sale, Victoria.

GINGER:

Ginger is a stylish girl. She likes children, other dogs, and even cats! Ginger loves cuddles and a good run between drop-offs. Could she be your new bestie? You can meet her near Frankston.

ARCHIE:

Do you have a warm front seat I could lie on? I'm an old guy and I don't need much, just some sunshine and the wind in my ears. And maybe the occasional scratch. I'd love to be your truck buddy. I'm in Sale if you're ever passing.

She looked at the ten profiles. It was a start, and if all went well, they could soon add more dogs. She took a deep breath, held her finger above *Upload* and pressed.

Then she sent a text to Anika.

'Trucker and Dog Matchmaking' is now live!

She shared the good news with Dad and Molly, then spent the rest of the evening waiting for replies.

CHAPTER 18
NEW YEAR FIRESTORM

The weather forecasters were right about the scorching weather. On Saturdays, she and Dad normally drove to the farmers' market for fresh supplies. Then they went to the bakery for a milkshake and coffee. This week, with thick smoke and dangerous wind gusts, they didn't hang around town. She checked the Trucker and Dog Matchmaking website every hour, but there were only a few hits; most of them probably from her and Anika.

The next day the temperature soared above one hundred and five. The news showed more images of kangaroos fleeing monstrous walls of flame and koalas approaching firefighters for water. She tried not to watch the burnt animal scenes, but she couldn't stop herself.

There were some positive stories too, though. Animal lovers across Australia were welcoming wild creatures into their homes. Volunteers were saving koalas and leaving sweet potato for endangered rock wallabies, and all around the world, people were knitting mittens and sewing pouches for burnt wildlife.

"Is your friend in Strathbogie okay?" Dad asked when he came back from helping to clear a neighbor's gutters.

"Anika said their area's safe, but the smoke's really thick. She wanted to know if we were all right. I said yes—but are we? It seems like the fires are coming closer."

"We're still okay, and we've got a fire plan—"

"Has anyone sent a message about adopting a dog?" she said.

Dad checked his phone and shook his head.

"We could send a call-out on the UHF channel."

"Let's wait till we get through the next few days." He looked preoccupied. "At the moment everyone's worried about bushfires."

Scout was impatient to match dogs, but he was right. Some people had lost everything. Others were busy fundraising. She went to sort the rocks she'd found during Operation Dog Food. As they tumbled, she rearranged the posters on her wall. Then she heard Dad shout, "You beauty! Australia wins the Test!"

She couldn't believe it. How could anyone get that excited about cricket?

They took a picnic dinner to Woolshed Falls, hoping the air would be better beside the waterfall, but it was just as hot and dusty. They ended up eating in the truck.

That night Scout couldn't sleep. Her bedroom was stifling, but it was too smoky to open a window. When the magpies warbled at dawn the morning sun looked like a creepy orange eye peering through red-brown smog. She carried Molly out to do her business and came straight back inside. She touched the shell in her pocket, trying to ignore the worried feeling in her belly.

But the breakfast news made her more nervous.

"Total fire bans have been declared in ten areas of New South Wales with gusty winds strengthening to an average of thirty to forty miles per hour. Wagga Wagga, one of the state hot spots, is expecting one hundred and eight degrees."

"Poor Sal," said Dad. "When will this extreme flippin' weather end?"

"In other regions, the fire at Mallacoota is generating its own weather. Residents of east Gippsland are urged to evacuate if it's safe to do so. Those seeking shelter should proceed to the Mallacoota jetty. If the situation worsens, CFA firefighters will create a wall of water to shield people. This fire is catastrophic."

Scout remembered the beautiful forest highway and

the creeks named after wombats and bellbirds.

"The Princes Highway east of Bairnsdale is closed and it is now too late to leave. Take immediate action to defend your life and property. There will be another update in fifteen minutes."

The phone rang and Dad answered. "G'day, Sal. Looks like you're in for some horror weather."

Silence. Then he added, "Are you sure?" And then, "Okay. Let us know if there's anything we can do to help."

"Is Aunty Sal okay?"

"Yes, her crew's been called to help with the fire near Corryong."

Scout remembered her nightmare image of Aunty Sal surrounded by flames. "Does she have to go?"

"Try keeping her away." Dad raised his eyebrows. "Sal and her crew are already halfway there."

"But this fire looks so dangerous."

"Sal won't take any risks."

"Neither did that man who died when the firestorm flipped his truck."

Dad frowned. "I think we need to stop watching the news."

"But then how will we know what's happening with Aunty Sal in Corryong?"

"Okay, let's do our chores and then tune in again

later. How's your scrapbook coming along?"

She showed him the "Molly Comes Home" page.

"I love that photo."

"Me too."

A few hours later Dad's phone rang again.

"Hey, Jillo, That's good, yeah, We're okay too." He stopped—almost as if he was checking mentally. "Scout's right here. I'll put her on."

"Hi, Scout, it's Jillo. I've been looking at your new website. All the dogs look nice, but Dotty is definitely the girl for me."

"That's great. I thought she'd be the one. You and Dotty are our first match!"

"Wonderful. Now what do I need to do next? I'm dropping a load in Melbourne next week, so I'll be near Dotty's shelter—"

Scout gave her Tony's details and said, "After you collect Dotty, can you send me a photo of her sitting in Pink Lady? We want to include good news stories on our site."

"Of course."

As soon as Jillo hung up, Scout sent a message to Anika.

Our first match!
   Dotty's been adopted.
   By a really nice lady.
   I think they'll be perfect for each other.
   After the New Year let's upload another dog.
Scout

She looked through her scrapbook. But which dog would she add to the website? Then she listened to an audio book and fell asleep. It was another restless night. She kept seeing Aunty Sal out in the forest fighting walls of fire.

Scout tried to think about Dotty riding in Pink Lady as she tossed and turned. But when she did, bolts of dry lightning flickered around Jillo's truck and the Dotty in her imagination was terrified.

The last day of the year was another scorcher. Fireworks were canceled in towns right across Australia. Scout kept checking Dad's phone for an update from Aunty Sal, but there were no messages. She hoped she was okay.

Dad asked if she wanted to invite Sam and his family over for a New Year sundowner.

"Can we just spend it together instead?" She liked Sam's family, but didn't want to farewell this sad year with other people. "How about we watch TV and I make a pavlova?"

"No worries. Sounds eggcellent."

She let the joke go.

As she whisked egg whites, she listened to the radio.

"Staff of the Mogo Zoo have ignored fire evacuation orders and remained to defend hundreds of animals from apocalyptic conditions. The lions and tigers stayed in their night dens while smaller animals were moved to safe houses. The zoo director even sheltered red pandas in his own home. Thanks to staff diligence, no zoo animals have been lost."

"That's some good news among all this horror," Dad said. But the next story was worse.

"In other news, thousands of people are gathered at the Mallacoota foreshore, waiting for the fire to pass. As the fire reached town, the blood-red sky became dark as night. People wore water-soaked shirts to cover their faces as ash rained down. Some residents have fled to sea in dinghies."

"It's like a sci-fi end-of-the-world horror story." Dad was shaking his head.

His phone rang. Scout left the egg whites to reach out and answer, hoping it was a trucker looking for a dog.

"Bill Galloway's phone—"

"Hello, my name's Jan. I'm calling from Wodonga Hospital. Can I please speak to Bill?"

"This is Bill's daughter."

"Is your father there?"

"Daaaad!"

As he took the phone, she gripped the scallop shell.

"Yes." He nodded. "I understand. Is she all right?"

Straining to hear, Scout leaned closer to the phone.

"Okay." Dad finished the call and turned to her. "Don't get worried, but Sal's been taken to hospital. Suffering from smoke inhalation and a possible broken arm. Her truck was caught in a fire-storm and hit a tree. She's waiting for an X-ray."

"Are you sure that's all?" Scout felt the nightmare flare up again. "She's not burnt or anything? We can't lose Sal too."

"She's all right." Dad hugged her. "It's just her arm. The nurse said Sal will call us as soon as she knows more."

Scout lay on the floor beside Molly and buried her face in her furry neck.

CHAPTER 19
BURRUMBUTTOCK

Sal's arm was fractured. With rest the doctor said it should be fine, but she'd also inhaled a lot of toxic smoke, so she needed oxygen to help her lungs recover.

"Being in hospital is driving me mad," she told them. "I need to get back out and help my crew."

"I want to help too," Scout said. "I'm sewing joey pouches as fast as I can."

But she was tired. During the day she couldn't stop thinking about the thousands of bush creatures that had died and at night she was still having nightmares. She researched ways to rehabilitate injured animals. Caring for them took months, so she sewed faster and concentrated on her stitching to try and take her mind off burnt koalas.

Dad left the emergency radio channel on, and her Top Hits program was constantly interrupted with updates.

"Around three thousand tourists and one thousand locals remain stranded in Mallacoota with conditions too dangerous to airlift them to safety. Residents say the red sky is terrifying. A naval ship is waiting offshore to evacuate the most vulnerable.

"And now, let's hear from our listeners," the presenter said. "We have Gina on the line. She breeds Murray Greys on a farm near Corryong. Thanks for your patience, Gina. Please go ahead."

Scout turned up the volume. Corryong was where Aunty Sal hurt her arm.

"Our burnt paddocks are like a black moonscape," the woman said in a shaky voice. "And our cattle are starving. If anyone can spare a bale of hay, please help us. We're desperate." She began crying as the presenter cut in.

"Thank you, Gina. I'm so sorry. Stay on the line and we'll get your contact details—"

The flyscreen door banged. Dad stepped in, wiping his greasy hands on a rag.

"I've sorted Big Rig's oil leak." He stared at Scout's face. "Okay, what's wrong?"

"There was a lady on the radio talking about starving cattle," she whispered. "The bushfires burnt their hay and they haven't got any food. I wish we could do something to help."

"As soon as the fires are out we'll contact Blaze Aid. They'll need volunteers to clear rubbish and repair fencing."

"Maybe we can take in injured animals."

"Yep, we could do that. But first we need to learn how to care for them properly."

He peered over her shoulder. "That roo pouch looks good."

"Thanks," she said. "My third one today."

"Good for you. I'll check the sprinklers, then let's make a big salad for lunch."

Scout folded the joey pouch and wondered how long a wildlife carer course would take to complete.

After lunch she tried something new. Aunty Sal's pattern for koala mittens didn't look hard, but they had to be made from one hundred per cent cotton. She found a worn tea towel in the sewing basket. She checked the tag. It was all cotton. As she cut the soft fabric, she imagined a koala paw nestling inside each semi-circle.

When Dad came back she handed him his phone. "Your mobile's been pinging."

He listened to his messages. "It's the Burrumbuttock Hay Runners."

"Burrum Who?"

"A group of truckers. They take donated hay to communities in drought."

"And you're not going to make a joke about their name?"

"Not today."

"Okay." She stopped laughing to herself. "So what did they want?"

"They're doing a special hay run to Corryong."

"Where the cattle are starving?"

"That's right. The farmers are desperate for feed and the Hay Runners have got stockpiles of donated hay. They want to deliver it before the weather gets worse, but they need trucks and drivers."

"Are you going to volunteer?"

"I'd like to, but someone needs to stay here to be with you. I don't know whether Sal's well enough to drive over."

"I could come with you in the truck—"

"It's too dangerous." Dad shook his head. "The winds are shifting all over the place."

"Then why are you going?"

"Scout, if I'm going to help, I need to be in Burrumbuttock ready to load before dusk."

"This afternoon?"

"That's right. In about four hours. The convoy leaves early tomorrow morning at five. Police will escort the trucks through highway blocks to Tallangatta. There'll be a fire truck and a water escort the rest of the way to

Corryong. After unloading, the drivers have to return the same day."

"I'm almost twelve. I could stay home by myself."

"Not in catastrophic fire conditions, you can't!"

"Okay, but you should help."

"Yep. That's what I think, too. Let's ask Sal. If her arm's okay and she leaves Wagga early, she can meet us in Burrumbuttock at 4.30 in the morning. As long as she's well enough, I reckon she'll agree. She knows better than most people what they're going though in Corryong."

"What about Molly?"

"Well, she's a truck-dog now. If Sal's able to help, Molly can sleep with us in the truck tonight at Burrumbuttock. We'll load the hay this evening. Then in the morning, you, Sal, and Molly can watch the convoy leave."

"What do you think?" Scout said to the dog.

Molly wagged her tail and shuffled closer.

"Looks like it's decided."

Dad sent Sal a text. Her arm was improving and she wanted to help.

"I'll be there by 4.30," Sal promised, "and tell Scout to bring her swimsuit. We can have a swim at the lake after you're on your way."

While Dad contacted the Hay Runners, Scout sent a message.

Hi Anika,

Guess what? Dad's joining a convoy of trucks taking hay bales to starving cows near Corryong. My aunty Sal was fighting fires there. She hurt her arm but it's getting better.

I'm not allowed to go with him, he says it's too dangerous, the convoy has to be escorted by police and a fire truck. But Dad's letting me go as far as Burrumbuttock, so I'll get to see the trucks being loaded. Molly's coming along too.

I've got to get ready. I'll send photos tomorrow.

Bye, Scout

"Right," Dad said as he put down the phone. "Thunderbirds are go."

She nodded. It was a weird saying from some TV show he used to watch in the olden days.

"We're being philanthropic again," she told him. "It's a good feeling!"

He ruffled her hair. "Your mom would be so proud."

"You know I won't be any trouble if I come with you—"

"I know, but the police wouldn't let you through their roadblock. The Hay Runners have special permission, but only for essential drivers. Coming as far as Burrum is the best I can offer."

Scout thought about the hungry cattle. She was glad Dad would be part of the convoy, even if she wasn't allowed to be.

"Okay."

"Good girl. The Hay Runners are doing another convoy to Armidale at the end of January. We could both go on that one if you want to, but in the meantime, if we're going to be there in time, I'll need your help."

While he attached a flat tray to the rig, she made ham sandwiches, cut a watermelon into cubes, and wrapped thick slabs of fruitcake. She put the containers of food into a cool bag with freezer blocks.

"What a feast," he said when he saw the food.

"I made extra so that you can leave some fruitcake and watermelon with the firefighters. I've also filled flasks with rainwater and put them on the veranda. What do you want me to pack for tonight's dinner?"

"How about we grab Indian takeaway as we go through Chiltern?"

"That sounds good! What else do we need to do?"

He checked his watch. "I'll water the garden, while you gather the washing. Can you do that?"

"Yep, I'm onto it."

They couldn't hang clothes outside because of the smoky air, so they were hanging around the house.

Scout folded everything then they left mid-afternoon to make sure they'd arrive in plenty of time. The organizers wanted to load as many trucks as they could before dark.

After driving with a full load on the dog food run, the sound of Big Rig's flat tray bouncing was strange. They crossed the Murray River floodplain and stopped near Howlong to eat their samosas and curry. Dad made the usual "how long?" jokes.

"Burrumbuttock is a small town with a big trucking heart," he said as they passed a tiny bush school like the one Scout used to go to. They turned at the Wirraminna Environment Center and saw rigs of all sizes gathered on the local footy oval.

"Wow," she cried. "I didn't know there'd be so many."

"They reckon there are more than fifty in the convoy."

He waved to the truckers he knew. Some rigs were already loaded. The organizers gave them a dashboard sign that read Truck #37 and Big Rig waited in line for their hay. While Dad was asking questions about weight and whether the bales were wet or dry, Scout saw a boy and girl climbing a tree on the edge of the oval. The girl waved so she waved back. They looked about the same age as her.

"Can I go and play with those kids?"

Dad nodded and she ran over.

"Are you part of the convoy?" they said.

"Yep, number thirty-seven."

The girl pointed to a huge semi-trailer. "That's our dad's truck. He's number twenty. I'm Ruby and he's Eli."

"We're twins," the boy added. "And we live in Burrumbuttock."

He wiggled his bum and Scout giggled. "Can I climb the tree with you?"

"Sure. If you put your foot on that branch it's easy."

"Are you going in the convoy?" said Ruby.

"No." Scout frowned. "I'm not allowed. How about you?"

"Nup—but we'll follow the trucks to Wodonga with our mom."

"My aunty said we can follow as far as the lake."

"Lucky!"

A forklift driver stacked bale after bale onto Big Rig's open tray as Dad shouted instructions, "Keep going. I reckon she can take a few more."

Hay was still being loaded onto trucks a few hours later when Scout fell asleep in her bunk.

CHAPTER 20
CORRYONG HAY RUN

The rumble of engines crept into Scout's recurring bushfire nightmare. She squinted into the smoky darkness. Dad was sitting in the driver's seat, checking his watch.

"What's the time?"

"It's 4.30. Sal should be here by now—"

She scrambled out of her bunk and sat next to Molly in the passenger seat.

The minutes ticked by. At 4.45 the trucks began moving into formation.

"Where are you, Sal?" Dad tapped the steering wheel. Then his mobile rang.

"Sorry, Bill." Sal sounded worried. "I left in plenty of time, but Hattie punctured a tyre just north of Culcairn. Some idiot didn't clear the road after a bingle."

"Are you okay?"

"Yes, but it took ages to change the tyre with one arm in the dark. I'm still thirty minutes away."

"The convoy's about to leave. Highway Patrol's standing by to escort us through Albury–Wodonga."

"Okay, how about I cut across through Thurgoona and wait by the road at Ebden? You could pull over near Boathaven."

"Great idea. Thanks, Sal, we'll see you there." He turned to Scout. "Well it looks like you and Molly will be coming along for the first part of the trip after all."

"Bonus!" Scout high-fived Molly's front paw. As the drivers revved their motors, horsepower grumbled through the air. The noise was deafening. Scout loved it.

They took position between Murray Rambler and Just Do It, both fully loaded Kenworth trucks like Big Rig. Burrumbuttock townsfolk lined the dark streets, waving torches, and cheering as the convoy rolled past.

"What a sight." Dad adjusted their dashboard number and sat up straighter. He looked proud and even a little teary. She couldn't see the front of the convoy through the bushfire haze, but she could certainly hear it.

At the edge of town, four kids in pajamas were standing in the back of a utility truck beside the road. Solar lights lit their hand-painted sign saying, "Good on you, Truckers!"

Scout reached across to toot the air horn. Then she held Molly by the window so that she could see too.

"Thanks for letting me come, Dad."

"I'm glad you're here. But only as far as Boathaven!"

She waved to the people waiting by the highway to cheer the trucks. "Let's toot the horn again."

Dad honked the air horn. The well-wishers yelled even louder.

While he chatted to truckers on the UHF channel, Scout reached for the sandwiches she'd packed. The early start had made her hungry. She offered him one.

"No thanks. The Country Women's Association ladies came round in the night with coffee and toast."

The sky lightened as their police escort led the trucks along the Hume Highway, but Scout could barely see the sun through all the smoke. Big Rig and the other rigs eased through Wodonga. One of the police officers at a roadblock gave Scout a thumbs-up. She waved and sat up proudly.

As they left the suburbs, Dad moved up through the gears and she settled back to enjoy the ride. Soon the convoy was hurtling along, making good time toward Lake Hume, where Sal should be waiting. Scout secretly hoped Hattie would get another flat tyre so she could go all the way to Tallangatta and Corryong.

The phone rang. It was Sal.

"I'm waiting by the highway just before the trailer park. There's space to pull over once you pass Hattie."

"Thanks, Sal!"

After the turnoff to Lake Hume's dam wall, Scout saw an orange car parked up ahead in the distance.

"There she is!"

Dad lifted the UHF mike. "Big Rig to Murray Rambler and other rigs behind Truck #37—"

"Go ahead, Big Rig."

"I'm making a two-minute stop at the campervan access road to drop off my daughter. I'll pull aside slowly so you can pass, then I'll re-join at the end."

"Copy that, Big Rig. It's Murray Rambler, no rush we'll ease back and give you space to re-join and keep position. Over."

Scout heard dozens of truck gears shifting down.

"Be ready to move quickly," Dad told her.

"Not a problem."

He pulled into the siding, letting Big Rig's engine idle as she hopped down from the rig, then reached up to take Molly.

"Thanks, Dad, I love you. Take care," Scout shouted as Big Rig moved back into formation.

"Love you too, Possum. Thanks, Sal."

Scout gave her aunty a huge hug then waved as Dad joined the other rigs. She was bursting with pride.

The convoy stretched forever!

"On ya, fellas," Sal shouted as the rigs passed. She knew a lot of the truckers, so there was heaps of tooting.

When the last truck had thundered past, Scout carried Molly to a shady tree and sat beside her aunt.

"How's your arm?"

"It's fine, just a hairline fracture. Everyone's making a fuss over nothing," Sal growled. "The quack told my fire crew I need to rest, but I hate not being able to help."

"You're helping us."

Her aunty smiled and pointed to an ice-cream van setting up for the hot day ahead.

"I know it's early," Sal said, "but I could demolish a strawberry nut sundae."

"Double-dip cone for me, please."

While they waited for their ice-creams, Scout touched Sal's red, scratchy face. "What happened?"

"A spot fire tried to fry me," Sal said.

"Wow, how close were you?"

"Too close."

"We were worried about you." Scout tilted her cone. The ice-cream was melting faster than she could lick. She put some on her finger for Molly, then crunched into her cone.

Aunty Sal finished her sundae, tied a scarf across her nose to block the smoke, and they found a good place to lay back on their towels. After their snack settled they paddled in the water. Scout floated on her back looking up into the strange red smog. Then she swam out to one of the drowned trees, while Sal and Molly lazed in the shallows.

How would it feel to be a fish — covered in hundreds of shining scales?

Scout duck-dived into the deeper water then swam back, shook fine white ash off her towel and lay down.

"How far away is Corryong?" she said.

"Just over sixty miles."

"The fire must be huge if we're getting ash all the way down here."

Aunty Sal nodded and looked sad.

"It is," she said.

Driving back to the farm in Hattie was exciting. People stared whenever Sal revved the engine, which she did a lot. Scout giggled and even Molly seemed to enjoy the attention. They sang along to the radio until a news update interrupted the music.

"In this bulletin there are fears that bushfires burning in the north-east could merge into a super blaze. Firefighters are bracing for extreme weekend weather with massive fires still raging in Corryong."

"Don't worry." Sal reached across to pat Scout's hand. "The convoy has a fire truck escort and your dad won't be going anywhere near the fire front."

The news on the south coast was also frightening.

"Small communities, including Cann River, are running out of supplies. Plans are underway to airdrop food, water, and satellite phones."

"We stopped at Cann River," Scout whispered. "The forest there was beautiful and we passed a creek named after wombats." She paused. "What do wombats do in a fire?"

"Don't worry about those guys," said Sal. "They're the bulldozers of the bush. Their tunnels go deep underground and they build lots of entrances. As long as wombats are near their burrow, they'll be fine."

"There was also a Bellbird Creek. What do bellbirds do in a fire?"

"Don't know," Sal said softly.

At home they kept busy. Scout showed Sal her scrapbook and they added a few extra stickers to the cover page. Then they sewed more mittens for burnt wildlife and Scout helped Sal cook zucchini fritters for dinner. Dad rang mid-afternoon. "We got through safely."

"Thank goodness. Are you okay, Dad? Was it scary?"

"It was terrible, but we delivered the hay." He was quiet for a moment, then he coughed and said, "We're about to head back. I'll tell you more later."

"We've made fritters for dinner."

"Sounds good. I'm at least two hours away, but I'll text when I'm past Yackandandah."

"Okay, see you." She turned to her aunty. "What'll happen if the weather does get worse this weekend? Will we be safe?"

"Don't you worry, love. Bill has everything ready. And hey," she flexed her good arm, "don't forget that I'm a fire-fighter. We'll be right, but I think I'll stay with you guys until the weather settles down, just to be sure." She squeezed Scout in a one-armed hug. "C'mon, let's go and fill up the water bowls. This smoke'll be making the animals thirsty."

As soon as the bird bath was full, rosellas flew down to drink, while a huddle of bees crowded the shallow watering station.

"Poor things," Scout said. "Flying through smoke must be terrible."

She sat with Molly watching the bees and rosellas while Sal checked Dad's fire-fighting pump. Then they pottered around the garden, raking leaves, and tidying up.

Toooot! Big Rig was coming down the track. Scout ran to open the gate.

Dad looked exhausted and the rig's undercarriage was covered in ash.

"Let's get you inside and fed," Sal said. "Scout and I will rinse the rig after dinner."

Dad was too exhausted to argue. He answered their questions, but Scout could see he didn't want to tell her the worst of it.

"You said it was bad up there, Sal, but I had no idea."

Aunty Sal nodded and changed the subject, telling him about the mittens they'd made for koalas. Scout knew from the glances between them, that with the catastrophic weather forecast for the weekend, things might soon become a lot worse. She clutched her scallop shell.

CHAPTER 21
EMBER ATTACK

They woke to thick smoke, scorching temperatures, and chilling bushfire news.

"Heat records continue to rise across Australia, and Sydney is expecting its hottest day ever. Residents in alpine communities hold grave fears that out-of-control fires will meet, turning high-country areas into an inferno. Mallacoota is under threat again, with extreme temperatures and high winds predicted. In Eden, hundreds of people must choose between defending their homes and fleeing as a massive fire moves toward town."

"I hope Meili and the other dogs are all right," Scout whispered.

"Their new owners will be taking good care of them."

So many bushfires were burning in areas they'd visited, and further across the country.

"In South Australia, the situation on Kangaroo

Island has worsened. Further west, the Eyre Highway is still closed, causing havoc for travelers."

"Poor Jabba," Dad said. "He's probably still stuck out there."

He switched off the radio. Saturday was their going to town day. They needed groceries, but with the choking air and wind gusts, he was reluctant to leave the farm.

"You and Scout duck into town," Sal said. "Molly and I can keep an eye on things here. I'll call if I need you."

"You sure?"

"Everything's bushfire ready."

"Okay, we'll be as quick as we can."

The shops were busy and the toilet paper shelves were bare again.

"Lucky we've got plenty at home." Dad grinned.

They grabbed essentials, then bought take-away drinks and donuts at the bakery. On the way home Dad stopped at the post office. He left the engine running while Scout checked their mailbox. There was a parcel from Tui. She opened it as they headed for home.

Hi Scout,
I hope you and Bill are safe.
Sorry I haven't replied sooner. Bushfire prep has kept me busy.

We're fine and so are the animals. Temporary carers are minding them until the danger has passed. There are so many thoughtful people in this world.

I love your website idea and Fly says he'd love to be a truck-dog. So do the mischievous kelpie pups and Archie the spaniel. Their carers have given them a bath and I've enclosed cute photos.

Remember we spoke about talismans? After you left, I was at the op shop buying old towels to use as dog rugs and I saw a bag on the counter with small unpolished stones. The lady said they might be semi-precious. My stingray tattoo gave me a tingling feeling so I decided it was worth investing $10 to find out. My uncle was a miner at Lightning Ridge and I think one of the stones is a tiny opal. Did you know that opals are good for creativity and self-worth?

Maybe this can be your special talisman, if you haven't already found one.

Cheers for now,

Your friend, Tui

Scout didn't know much about opals, she'd never seen a real one, but she did know that they held different colors, called "fire."

"Are Tui and her animals safe?" Dad wondered.

"The dogs are with carers until the bushfires pass. Look, Tui's sent me some stones to polish. One might be an opal."

"Wow, that's generous."

At home they ate donuts with Sal, then Scout tipped the rough stones onto the table, guessing straightaway which one Tui thought was an opal.

"Hey, Dad, is it okay if I do some rock tumbling?"

"Sure, we need to stay inside anyway, out of that toxic air."

She set up her tumbler. She couldn't wait to see if Tui's stingray was right. Hours later she opened the lids, shook out the grit and held her breath. Would the little stone turn out to be a talisman?

Blue and green glinted among the brown.

It was an opal!

One part of the stone was still rough and she knew that if she polished any more, the opal would break. She ran her fingers over the blue-green sparks. The stone was like a miniature rainbow. And there was even one speck of red, the most precious opal color.

She sewed a scrap of leftover fabric from one of Mom's dresses into a tiny pouch, then tucked the opal inside. That night she put the pouch under her pillow and her dreams were peaceful. It was as if the opal's fire came from a tiny dragon that kept infernal nightmares at bay.

Dad flicked off the morning news as Scout walked into the kitchen.

"What were you watching?" she said.

"Footage from the high country. It's probably better not to see it."

"Why?"

"The fire fronts are joining. They showed animals fleeing. Not all of them made it."

She rubbed her eyes. "There are so many heartbreaking photos online and on TV."

He opened his arms. "Come here, Possum."

"All those burnt animals." She nestled into Dad's chest and sobbed. "Someone on the radio said that over a million could have died."

He stroked her hair.

"Let's play Scrabble, or Monopoly. You choose."

They both played board games with Sal all afternoon. They finished a five hundred piece jigsaw and kept the news off. In the evening Scout said she was okay and that she wanted to know what was happening. "Even if it's terrible."

The update showed bushfire devastation across the country.

"The fire came within feet of us. We were down by the creek with wet towels—"

"I've never seen anything like it."

"After years of struggling through drought, everything we own has been burnt."

"The sky was terrifying."

"We had no idea whether we'd survive, until three heroes in the back of a utility truck came to help."

A reporter stood in the middle of burnt-out Batlow. Even their Big Apple was singed. But not everything was destroyed. Somehow the Rural Fire Service had rallied to defend the "undefendable" town. Then Scout saw a familiar face.

"It's Jai. He's on the news!"

"Yeah, they reckoned the town couldn't be saved." The wind pushed a dreadlock across Jai's sooty face. "But we all pitched in. Anyone who could hold a hose helped. We lost some buildings, but we saved a lot of others." The reporter asked Jai a question as the camera zoomed onto a car behind him. Scout saw a rusty colored heeler guarding animal crates. "Yep, the dog's safe in there. She's protecting some magpie chicks, a possum, and a puggle."

Jai laughed and Scout's heart did a little flip.

He'd saved the animals.

"Good on ya, Jai," Dad cried.

All week the fires devoured bushland. Thousands more animals died. Authorities said that a million had perished. Then they said five million. Or fifty million. No one really knew. Soon people were saying half a billion animals might have been lost. Hundreds of small charities worked around the clock to help.

Scout abandoned her Holiday Plan. Whether she did or didn't go to Arcadia seemed irrelevant now. There were more important things to worry about, like fresh fires breaking out and like trying not to breathe the toxic air. She sewed dozens of mittens with one-armed Sal as they listened for updates on a fire raging near Harrietville and Abbeyard. While they stitched, Molly practiced standing up. She was wobbly, but becoming stronger.

On Thursday, residents of Bright received automated texts. The Abbeyard fire was approaching and it was time for them to leave.

"Bright's forty miles away," Sal said. "We're still okay."

By Friday the bushfire was threatening Myrtleford and another grass fire had started south of Wodonga.

Sal frowned as she turned up the radio.

"Don't worry." She smiled, smoothing Scout's forehead. "We'll be fine. The wind isn't blowing our way."

Scout loved her aunty, but hated it when adults weren't completely truthful. She knew the wind was shifting all over the place.

They went to check that debris hadn't blown into the yard. While Dad filled the gutters with water, Sal hosed the roof.

"Just in case," she said.

"Should we evacuate?" Scout asked.

"Not yet. The Wodonga fire's moving east, not south toward us."

"But the app shows the Abbeyard fire is almost at Nug Nug. And that's only thirty miles away. What if it comes closer?"

"When the firefighters tell us to go, we'll go. In the meantime the gutters are full and the sprinklers are attached to the solar pump. We've got a solid fire plan."

"I'm frightened."

"I know." Dad stroked her cheek. "We all are, and

there'll be thousands of people across Australia feeling the same way. The important thing is not to panic. Can you do that for me?"

"I'll try."

"Dad's right," Sal added. "We're still at 'Watch and Act'. If that changes we'll head straight to the evacuation center."

Scout stroked the ridges of her scallop shell. They were all wearing masks, jeans, and long-sleeved merino undershirts, as well as farm boots and woollen socks. The temperature was over 100 degrees Farenheit. She was boiling.

Sal hosed Big Rig, the shed and the house, while Dad swept away leaves. Then he told Scout to go inside.

"But I want to be with you and Aunty Sal."

"Your job is to keep Molly calm," Aunty Sal said as she closed the doors and windows. "Take her into the laundry and make sure everything is by the door ready to grab if we need to go."

Scout went inside, but peeked through the laundry door, watching Dad hammer metal sheets around their veranda.

"Just in case." He mouthed the words, giving her a wave. Then he climbed onto the roof to cover their chimney.

Soon after, Sal's mobile rang.

"Okay," she shouted, "they're upgrading the alert. It's time to go."

Their emergency kit, with food and water, was already packed in Hattie's boot. Scout grabbed her bag of valuables. They were each allowed one backpack. She had her rock tumbler and favorite gems, photo albums, some things of Mom's and the "Operation Dog Food" scrapbook. The precious Christmas letter and opal were tucked inside a plastic bag in her jeans pocket.

Dad carried Molly to Hattie, and Scout ran ahead to open the gate. She looked back at their home, glad they were leaving, but terrified that it might not be here when they returned. Their house held so many precious memories of Mom.

"Leave the gate open for the firies!" Sal shouted.

As they raced along the track Scout saw water bombers in the distance. Sal's mobile pinged with updates. They stopped at a roadblock.

"A spot fire has broken out," the SES woman yelled. "You can't get through."

Sal spoke to the fire coordinator on her two-way. "The fire has jumped containment lines," she said. "The safest place for us now is back on the farm." Scout's legs trembled. "It's all right," Sal told her, "the fire front isn't near us, but we do need to watch for ember attack."

"You sure it's best to go back?" Dad asked.

Sal nodded. "They've told the water bombers we'll be at the house. They'll do a flyover and keep an eye on us."

The fires raged closer. As hot gusts shifted, the first embers flew into their yard. Aunty Sal scowled and hosed them down.

Scout peered out from the laundry. There was so much smoke.

"It's okay," she told Molly over and over, "Mom'll be watching over us."

Bits of ash danced around the house. Dad ran in to reassure Scout that everything would be fine. Then he raced back to join Sal, stamping on leaves, and embers and hosing the roof. The sky darkened and the wind howled. Scout tried to be brave.

She held a wet cloth over Molly's nose then lay on the floor beside the whimpering terrier. They stared through the glass door at the shuddering gums. Branches shook leaves onto the ground faster than Dad could rake them up.

The dark clouds gathered. Scout chewed her lip, worrying about their rosella friends and the bees and lizards. Molly woofed. The wind had suddenly stopped. It was eerie. Scout stood up and stepped outside to peer into the angry sky.

"The wind's changed!" Sal yelled.

"Thank goodness!"

Dad hugged Scout and spun her around. Then she looked up. Fine mist was falling onto her face. "It's raining!"

They cheered. It was just a sprinkle, but enough to douse the embers. For now their home was safe. A perfect green leaf floated down from Mom's tree. Scout squeezed the talisman in her pocket and whispered "Thank you" to the sky.

CHAPTER 22
A NEW START

A week later the rosellas were back at the watering station. Scout searched the shallow bowls for bees, but couldn't find any. She went inside to check that everything was ready. Molly was wearing a ribbon. Her bedroom was tidy. She'd even dusted her rocks. Anika was coming for a sleepover and Scout couldn't wait. She looked at the clock. They should be here any minute.

After the ember attack, Dad had removed the protective metal sheets and now their house looked like a home again. Sal's arm was improving. She'd returned to Wagga and the doctor said she could even drive Firebird again. Last they'd heard, she was inland, somewhere near Dubbo.

Scout peered out the window. No dust cloud on the track yet.

While she waited she covered her schoolbooks with contact paper. She'd decided to follow Mom's advice and go back to Arcadia. Hopefully boarding school would be better with a friend.

Molly sniffed the contact.

"Look out or your nose will get stuck."

Her tail gave a lazy wag as she hobbled over to check for food scraps. She still couldn't walk far, but her hips were becoming stronger.

"How did Mom do this?" Scout smoothed out the air bubbles trapped under the contact, then listened to the radio and cut another sticky sheet.

"Defence Force personnel are evacuating residents on Kangaroo Island after new fire outbreaks. And in other news, Chinese officials are yet to identify what's causing an outbreak of pneumonia in the city of Wuhan. More news at midday . . ."

She remembered the ash swirling into their yard and shivered. Thank goodness the wind had turned in time. She crossed her fingers for the families on Kangaroo Island, then looked out the window. A dust swirl. At last! She ran to meet her friend, but when Anika waved, suddenly she felt shy.

A boy jumped out of the car and raced toward the Kenworth.

"Wow!" he hollered as Dad crawled out from under Big Rig.

Scout laughed and her shyness melted.

"That's my brother, Pran," Anika said, "and this is my mom."

"Hello, Mrs Kohli."

"Thank you for inviting us."

"How about a cup of tea?" Dad suggested.

"That would be lovely." Mrs Kohli held out a box. "I've brought some gulab jamun for Scout to try and some vegetarian samosas."

"That's kind of you."

Pran tugged his mother's sari. She sighed and said, "I'm sorry but I will have no peace until I ask whether my son could possibly sit in your truck."

Dad grinned. "Of course. Maybe after our cuppa he'd like to go for a ride down to the road and back?"

Pran looked like he'd burst with excitement.

"Okay, you heard Mr Galloway. Now go and run around while we have our tea."

"Scout's treehouse is over there," Dad suggested.

As Pran scrambled up the tree Mrs Kohli frowned. "Two weeks ago he was a different boy, struggling to breathe that horrible air."

"So the smoke was bad at Strathbogie?"

"Terrible, but nothing like what some communities are facing. And you had a frightening time here."

Scout grabbed Anika's hand and whispered, "Let's go and find Molly."

After they'd fussed over the dog, Scout showed Anika her "Operation Dog Food" scrapbook, then they checked their website. Anika had updated Rusty's profile after Jai and Rusty appeared on television. She'd added a link to the news clip and put stars on a banner saying, "Hero Dog". Rusty had received dozens of hits and was adopted the next day.

"How cute is Jai!" Anika sighed.

"So cute."

"And brave."

They watched the news clip again, then Scout told Anika that Tui had sent photos of three more dogs.

"Let's upload them."

Anika looked at the photos and they began writing rescue dog bios.

"Lunch!" Dad's homemade chutney was perfect with Mrs Kohli's samosas and salad leaves from their garden.

"Please take a jar of chutney home with you," he offered.

Scout tried the gulab jamun. It was super-sweet but delicious. Then Dad winked at Pran.

"Okay, young fella, let's fire up the Kenworth."

Pran loved Big Rig's air horn. After their third lap, tooting around the property Mrs Kohli said she'd better take him home.

The sleepover was fun. They smashed a pile of geodes and Anika polished some rocks to take home. Dad drove them into town for milkshakes and they swam at Woolshed Falls with Sam. Showing Anika her favorite places made them feel even more special.

When they dropped Anika back at Strathbogie, Mr and Mrs Kohli told Scout she was welcome to visit anytime.

"Maybe you'd like to come and stay one weekend after school goes back."

Scout glanced at Anika. She was nodding.

"Thanks, that'd be great!"

A few days later Scout was getting ready to leave for boarding school.

"Hey, Dad," she said as she stuck a picture of Ron and Hermione onto the cover of her new maths workbook. "I've got a joke for you."

"Okay."

"What do you call a dog that becomes a wizard?"

"I don't know."

She pressed out the last air bubble with a ruler. "A labracadabrador!"

"That's even worse than your joke about the police

sniffer dog." He laughed and put fruit and a box of homemade biscuits by the door. "Are you all packed?"

She tucked the workbook into her bag. "Ready to roll!"

He checked his watch. "Let's have one more look at your scrapbook before we skedaddle."

They turned the pages, pointing to photos and smiling at favorite memories from Eden, Batlow, and Ninety Mile Beach.

"Operation Dog Food was a great trip," Dad said as a pretty leaf blew through the open window.

"It was the best," she said. She stroked Molly's ears, then reached across to give her dad a huge hug. "And I think the three of us are going to be okay."

Dad ruffled her hair and Molly licked her hand as a leaf floated onto her scrapbook. Scout smoothed it between her hands, then tucked it safely between the pages.

PLACES SCOUT VISITS AND HEARS ABOUT

Adaminaby is home to the Big Trout sculpture. In 1956 the old town was shifted to its current location, making way for Lake Eucumbene, part of the Snowy Mountains Hydro Electricity Scheme. The original town lies below the waters of the lake.

Bairnsdale is home to a colony of threatened grey-headed flying foxes which help pollinate over 100 species of native trees.

Barnawatha is a small town by the Hume Highway. In recent years it's become a rail and trucking transport hub.

Batlow, a small town on the edge of the Great Dividing Range, is famous for apples and cherries.

Beechworth is a historic town in north-eastern Victoria. It was a wealthy gold mining area during the 1850s, attracting people from across the world, reflected in the multicultural cemetery with its tall

Chinese burning towers and pioneer graves. In 1885 an electoral candidate rode a horse with solid gold horseshoes and the bushranger Ned Kelly was imprisoned in Beechworth Gaol.

Bright is a pretty tourist town close to the Victorian Alps, famous for its colorful autumn leaves.

Burrumbuttock, affectionately known as Burrum, is a small town in the central Riverina. It's home to the philanthropic Burrumbuttock Hay Runners and the award-winning Wirraminna Environmental Center.

Corryong lies in the beautiful upper reaches of the Murray River. The grave of Jack Riley, the reputed "Man from Snowy River" from Banjo Paterson's famous poem, can be found in the local cemetery.

Ebden, population 136 (2016 census) is situated by Lake Hume.

Eden is a town on the New South Wales coast. It's famous for whale-watching during the May to early November migration and you can see Old Tom's skeleton at the museum.

Frankston Pier is 1640 feet (500 meters) long. It was built in 1857 then extended in 1864. Semaphore flags on the pier's support poles spell out a hidden message.

Gundagai is a historic town on the Hume Highway. Traditionally the wide flood plain was a meeting place for the Wiradjuri people. The famous Dog on the Tucker Box can be found about four and a half miles (seven kilometers) north at Snake Gully.

Lightning Ridge, the home of rare black opals, is a mining town in outback New South Wales.

Ninety Mile Beach is a 90 mile (150 kilometer) long stretch of golden sandy beach facing Bass Strait. In the sand you might see tube-building worms or tiny crabs.

Sale was an important Cobb and Co stagecoach town in the late 1800s (you can still see the old stables). As a gateway to the Victorian Alps, Gippsland Lakes and the Ninety Mile Beach, it's still a busy town.

Strathbogie is a small town in the Victorian Alps.

Tumblong village is tiny but travelers enjoy its wayside tavern.

Wagga Wagga means many crows/dance dance in the Wiradjuri language. The city lies beside the Murrumbidgee River. Wagga has been home to many sporting heroes and is the place where the Chiko Roll was created.

Wodonga is situated on the southern side of the Murray River, which separates Victoria and New South Wales. Albury is on the other side. Sometimes they're called twin cities.

Wollongong is situated south of Sydney and its name comes from the Dharawal word, woolyungah, which means five islands.

Woolshed Falls is a popular picnic and swimming place near the historic town of Beechworth.

Yarrangobilly Caves: There are several limestone caves to explore. The oldest ones are millions of years old, and you can float in thermal pools.

The Hume Highway links Melbourne and Sydney. It was named after the explorer Hamilton Hume, who, together with William Hovel, traveled between Sydney and Port Phillip (Victoria) in the early 1800s.

The Murrumbidgee River is part of the Murray-Darling Basin and it's Australia's second longest river. The name Murrumbidgee means plenty of water/big river in the Wiradjuri language.

The Princes Highway stretches over 1180 miles (1900 kilometers), passing through three states and connecting Sydney and Adelaide.

The Snowy Mountains Highway is a dramatic scenic drive in southern New South Wales. The east end links the New South Wales South Coast to the Monaro region. The west end gives access to the Snowy Mountains.

ACKNOWLEDGEMENTS

This story was written on Noongar Menang country in south-western Western Australia and Scout's journey takes her through the lands of many Traditional Owners, including; Waveroo, Taungurong, Woiworung, Boonwurrung, Kurnai, Bidwell, Yuin, Jaitmatang, Ngarigo and Wiradjuri. I pay my respects to the Traditional Owners of all the areas where Scout's story takes place.

Many people have helped bring this story to life. Thank you to my agent, Clive Newman, for helpful advice on early drafts and for finding the perfect home for this book. Enormous thanks to all the wonderful team at Walker Books, especially Christina Pagliaro, and also Jarred Noulton. I am deeply grateful for Mark Macleod's generous editorial coaching and coaxing. It was a privilege to work with Mark. His editorial wisdom taught this old dog new tricks, and took Scout's story to a whole new level. A special thank you to Tony Flowers, for the gorgeous cover, and for breathing life into the dogs. I want to take them all home!

Sophie Wolfer is the best editing daughter a writer could ever hope for. Thank you. Grateful hugs also to Karen Davidson, Audrey Davidson and Peter

Watson for insightful suggestions and feedback over many, many drafts. I'm so fortunate to have writing friends who have offered honest feedback along this journey. Special thanks to Deb Fitzpatrick and Kate Woodward for going above and beyond with editing advice, as well as Jane Witherow, Maree Dawes, Barbara Temperton, Emma Crook, Beth Kirkland and Sian Turner.

Truck drivers keep Australia functioning. You are our unsung heroes! Thank you to Menang Elder, Lester Coyne, for detailed trucker advice, and Margaret and Tiggy Gibson for descriptions of sleeping in a truck cab. I'm also grateful to Marg Sefton and the (2022) Year Six class at Parklands School, Albany, as well as Eden, Mason and Kristy Montgomery and Benjamin Ruett for helpful suggestions along the way.

The 2019/20 bushfires were dreadful beyond comprehension, with toxic air and terrifying scenes. My sister evacuated twice. My cousin's family traveled 93 miles (150 kilometers) from Murmungee to help fight the Corryong fires. Wildlife carers across the country gave their time selflessly. The generosity of the Burrumbuttock Hay Runners, and all who donated feed, saved the lives of countless animals. To the rescue center volunteers who spent time and money saving animals and sewing animal mittens and pouches, thank you. To the firies, SES and other emergency responders, thank you. To the people who held hoses and cared for displaced humans and wildlife, thank you. The kindness of everyday Australians has inspired Scout's journey.

Title selection can be a challenging business. Accolades to the brainstorm trust: Karen Davidson, Audrey Davidson, Sophie Wolfer, Peter Watson, Clive Newman, Mark Greenwood and Frané Lessac.

Finally, thank you, Pete for finding Harry among the gallery of rescue dog photos I sent so many years ago. You chose well! And tummy tickles for Harry the rescue boy for bringing so much joy into our home.